D1087907

THROUGH GLASS

AMERICAN LAND SERIES • VOLUME 1

THROUGH GLASS

A NOVEL BY HENRY ALLEY

IRIS PRESS, INC.

IRIS PRESS, INC.
27 Chestnut Street
Binghamton, New York 13905

Printed in the United States of America

Cover by Stuart McCarty

Library of Congress Cataloging in Publication Data

Alley, Henry, 1945–
Through glass.

(American land series; v. 1)
I. Title. II. Series.
PZ4.A4328Th [PS3551.L447] 813′.5′4 79-21296

ISBN 0-916078-06-X CLOTH
ISBN 0-916078-07-8 PAPER

FIRST EDITION

Second Printing

A GLADYS HARDEN STONE BOOK

Gladys Harden Stone is the first patron member of Iris Press, Inc., a non-profit publisher of literary works. Publication of this novel was made possible by a generous grant from Mrs. Stone in memory of her father,

Seaborn Judge Tecumseh Harden,
1871–1938.

ACKNOWLEDGMENTS

A special note of thanks to editors
Alexander P. Cappon of *The University Review*
and R. C. Halla of *The Riverbottom Magazine*,
whose journals first published my work.
Also, I am especially grateful to
James McConkey for his sustained
encouragement during the period of this
novel's formulation, from first stage to last.

FOR PATRICIA ALLEY

THROUGH GLASS

PART ONE

STAINS OF LIGHT

He stood at the window. The glass, in multiple reflection, took him out and away to the district of Jutland, the autumn district of chimney-like houses which rested on the Sound. It was as if, momentarily, he could see fall arriving like a fleet of invisible ships, hurrying through the canals, beneath the wrought iron bridges of Seattle, tilting the scales of the season, changing the angle of the sun.

It was the moment he had been waiting for: for as he turned from the window and lit the lamp above the desk, he was brought back to the reflections again. He saw his drafting table, or better, its ghost, duplicated infinitely; saw his tools, placed so carefully, above the blank page, with his own rolled diagrams set below, critically numbered and referenced, like mariner's charts in a Renaissance galleon. It was as if, momentarily, he was released from Jutland by the very design of his blueprints. Jutland, with its multiplicity and confusion—and only emblematic of the greater melee of Seattle itself—was refining itself slowly in the halo of the late afternoon, leaving only his brightly lit configurations. It was the arrival of the skeletal vision that his teachers had promised.

But why, then, was his father there with him? Years ago, his father had taken a single step from a ladder and vanished. And his mother, in the years following, had disappeared into another strange city. And now his father was there like a rankling ghost—imminent, threatening, and yet giving him strength. Together, they seemed to complete the settlement of the city's vista, and Jutland, which had finally received the bitter commitment of his father's ashes, no longer frightened him.

ONE

Toward four o'clock, his father called him into the back room—his office away from town. Ed, in the midst of packing, delayed some, so that by the time he got there, his father had gone back to his work. In the dim light, his face, bent above the desk, was fixed in puzzled concentration. Ed, hesitant, could not remember seeing the same look before. It changed the very structure of the room: its landscape of window views, west and north, of glassed shelves forming the upper body of his grandfather's bookcase—glass that was a veritable hearth squaring the sun through the webbing of the branches and leaves outside. Ed, standing in the doorway, could suddenly smell the burning peat in the air, the first promise of fall—and he could feel a line being drawn between him and the room he was about to enter. "It's all so steady," he said to himself. The room, combined with his father's office in town, had been a mainstay and, for all the years that Ed could remember, had enabled them to live very consistent, routine lives. And now everything was to be changed.

His father looked up, frightened. "I've had to change our plans," he said. "Could you be ready to go by tonight?"

"Tonight?" Ed asked. "There are still my books to pack, and I've got the draft board to call and a thousand other—"

"Do you remember Sam Webb?" his father asked.

"Of course."

"I've just gotten a letter from the Company saying they're going to take his store away from him."

"They can't do that."

"Yes, they can—they hold the loan—but that isn't the point. *Why* they should do it, when he's been depending on that loan—and buying the Company's shoes from me—is something I can't fathom." His father sat in silence for a moment, as if planning a counter-strategy. Ed noticed the map off to one side of the desk, in the square of sun. "Don't worry," his father said, still frightened. "We'll get you to Stanford all right. But I need to take a side trip to Eurkay to find out from Webb what the hell's going on."

"Couldn't you just call him?"

"There's no finding out that way." And Ed could see that there were other reasons, that his father must widen the trip to make way for more tension. But he was still bitterly disappointed. He could think of no plan of his that his father had not totally revised because of some pressing obligation. Out of ancestral design, his father carried his mule pack of troubles during work and vacation both. For nearly half a year, Ed had been planning otherwise—that his father would drive him in triumph to the California campus, that together they would enjoy what they had earned, if only momentarily, truly sustaining the heritage, mending the crack which ended, broke his grandfather's memoirs.

"Webb is a worthless freeloader," Ed said angrily. "He's used you for twenty years and now he's using us. You know I had everything planned."

"There's nothing I can do about it," his father answered. "If Webb tells me what I think—that they pulled the rug out for no reason—then I'll have to be on my way to St. Louis in four days."

"That's ridiculous!" Ed nearly shouted. "You know what the doctor told you, and you know what Webb *will say*—he'll say all those things just to set you off."

"There is nothing," his father went on—and he moved the map in Ed's direction—"that's going to spoil Stanford for you." He pointed to the route connection between the line of Eurkay Canyon and the main road. "We'll simply pick up the trip here, driving 100 miles back to the Coast, once we're done. Once I get you to Stanford, I'll drive back to Seattle, clear things up at the office and then fly out to St. Louis." His finger was moving along the interstates and then, mid-air, to St. Louis and the confrontation—as if all things could be explained, justified, as long as they were located.

"I'm not mad about Stanford," Ed insisted. "I'm just scared about you." And yet he was frightened, exposing himself like this. "You can't go through one of your marathons and come out all right."

"Can't you see," his father interrupted, sitting down again, "that I can read my own death warrant in this? Can't you, Ed?"

"No, I can't," Ed answered directly, but not fully responding. "No, I don't understand."

"Webb represents all of my accounts," his father said. "I've been building on him for thirty years. If I lose him, it's just the beginning of what the Company will take away from me."

"But surely they don't hold loans for all of your accounts."

"No," his father said, caught by the fact. But the admission only turned on him. "I think they—Elden Foley, I mean—are trying to humiliate me—they want to see how much I'll take."

"But why?"

His father, not answering, looked like the refined ghost of himself: austere, white-, almost silken-skinned. His face with its Roman nose was, in the shadow, like a profile cut on a silver coin, aged by two millennia and of inestimable value.

"I wish I could answer that question, Ed. But out here I only get part of the rumors. My one guess would be that everything is going to come under the heading of Consolidated. That would mean that all the color lines are going to be absorbed."

"That would mean yours would go," Ed said. "West Green wouldn't be yours."

"It's hard to think about. But that's what it would mean."

Ed thought of all the emblems—the tree, looking so much like a mountain ash—which starred his father's office. When he had been younger, he had always rummaged through his father's desk looking for the give-away balloons, whose trees he would blow to unbelievable size; the "G" of the West Green opening like a set of jaws, beside the widening, emerging branches of the flaming green. And now the office would be stripped of its emblems, right down to the West Green stickers, which, as a boy, he had carelessly licked and placed on every envelope in sight. Where were they now? They would become misplaced, antiquated, rare, as discarded and lustreless as the hotel sign framed in his father's sixth story window. Standing there, so close to his father and wanting to touch him, he could feel the room move ahead of him, out of reach, into the incipient autumn—as if he could forecast his father's failure along with his own, as if this were a forewarning of what would happen at the university.

"Is there anything I can do?" Ed asked finally. "Could I stay here and help you?"

"No, Ed, you have school. Besides, I have Jamison to help me."

"But you could let Jamison go—prove to the Company that you can run things cheaper—I wouldn't charge anything."

Ed knew he was speaking childishly, or out of innocence, but somehow his father was drawn. "I appreciate that, but that isn't what the Consolidated group is looking for. They want someone more high-powered, less regionally oriented. They know—Foley knows—Washington is all I've ever been good at, and they're going in the opposite direction. No, firing Jamison would be doing just what they're doing. Even though I'd like you here." His father stopped, hearing the door. A final slam. It was Ed's mother.

"What was that?" she called out, as if summoned. "Is Ed going to stay here with you?"

She was, within moments, coming toward them, her auburn suit scented faintly, through the perfume, with the bus ride home. She seemed to bring with her the lit auroras, rose-colored and smoke-haloed, of fall, the lumber-dark district where she worked all afternoon behind counters. It was as if the lens of the room were dimmed suddenly, as if she brought with her a flourish of autumn leaves—and the song which she played so flawlessly on the piano.

"So what are all the secrets?" she asked.

"I've been thinking about going to Eurkay first—then Stanford," his father said.

"To talk to Webb?"

"Yes—and if he isn't the one who prompted all this, I'm going to fly to St. Louis and have it out with Foley."

"So you're going to push yourself again," she said. "If you add Eurkay now, you'll have to leave tonight."

"Ed's almost ready."

She didn't answer, only stood rigidly beside him.

"It's all right," Ed told her. "It'll give us some extra time together."

"What about your draft board?" she asked angrily. "You have to be absolutely sure you have your waiver. I don't want you on some battlefield in Vietnam."

"For Christ's sake, Karin," his father said. "Don't be so morbid."

"You're the one who's morbid," she said. "How could you possibly spoil everything for Ed when he's been working toward this for four years? You could go to Eurkay after leaving him off at Stanford."

"But I have to get there now," his father insisted. "I have to know from Webb firsthand so I can decide what to do." And with the two of them standing in the doorway, he seemed to feel checkmated, conspired against; he fought off their glances at first by staring at the map and then irritably leaving the room. In a moment, Ed could hear him in the basement, banging suitcases and shoe sample grips.

"There's no changing him when he's like this," she said.

"You have no idea what he's like when he sets his mind to something. It's as if he's getting revenge." She looked about her, as if trying to avert the change, and then said, "Well, if you're going tonight, there's no way I can stop it. Give Marlice Webb my love and ask her if she still remembers Balboa Polytechnic. In fact—" and then her glance seemed to find the mainstay, the protection, she had been looking for—"you can ask her if she still has that graduation program she wrote me about."

"You mean when you were in San Francisco?"

"Yes," she said, laughing suddenly, "we went to high school together there."

"All right, I will."

"And so," she said, looking at the clock, "let's get both of you ready. Are you finished packing?"

"Mostly."

"All right," she said, smiling, "I'll go down and try helping your father."

Left to himself, Ed was taken by a slow isolation, like water through a chink. He wanted his mother to return and talk again about how his father had ruined everything—or remind him about the draft board. The moment was hard to stand up to—his mother leaving with a perfunctory kiss, and his father creating sounds of breakage in the basement, which would finally engulf the entire house. "I must get ready to leave," Ed told himself. "I mustn't stay here anyway." But as he stood there, staring at the bookcase, which was still reddened, polished with sun—he saw through to an image of his draft board clerk, sitting at her desk and kindly registering him. She was a woman, clearly, with children of her own—"just about his age," as they were often known to say. And now, suddenly, this woman seemed entirely dangerous—which he had never even considered her before—for behind her now stood an alien country, where his mother's voice had placed him.

Slowly he went over to the bookcase and took out his grandfather's memoirs, pocketed them for safe keeping—for himself.

TWO

The car stood idling, restless. Ed, leaning beside the open trunk and waiting for his father to come with the final pieces, looked up toward the front of the house and saw it as one of their friends had caught it—on blurry 1950's eight millimeter—in partial Kodachrome. And the house changed before him in all its seasons, with its cherry trees snowing gently, their blossoms gathering like heaps of dust or snow, and the wind forking over the wreckage, silver now, of the plants of the previous fall; with the clouds shattering or melting like ice crystals, or spiraling, in the shapes of cones or seashells, down to points or hearts of liquid blue, or gathering, as the brigades of a storm, about a single open window in the sky, the window becoming the crown of a dome as the rafters of light would begin to spread, as the whole zenith would change to the tints of a peace rose, opening.

And all about him, now, there were the sounds of the evening, gathering, rushing, ceaseless, like the descending sprays of a waterfall. There were the sounds of football players, practicing early on the field, the cries of children going down a slide, the rumble of scooters and wagons across the pavement, and the laughter of girls playing in attic rooms—the resounding collapse of a folding chair, the raising of a sash.

"Well, Ed, that's it," his father told him, coming out. "I almost forgot my nitroglycerin pills"—and placed a small case carefully into the trunk.

"And here's the phone number of your draft board," his mother said. "You'll have to call them from the Webbs since you can't get them here. Now is there anything that you've forgotten?"

"Not that I can think of."

"Then you'd better be off," she said, perfunctory again. "And you," she said to his father. "Since you're going to Eurkay, settle this with Webb here and now—forget about St. Louis. You know he isn't worth fighting for."

"Well we don't have time for another argument," his father said good-humoredly. The two of them, like some emblem of a shy couple, some fifty-five years old, cast in the bronze molding of the sun, gave each other a shy kiss.

"Do you have your nitroglycerin?"

"Yes, yes."

"Do you have your draft board number?"

"Yes, Mom—see, Dad, she wants us to blow the board up!"

"Very funny."

Raucous laughter, while they moved off, escaping any emotional opportunity.

His father raised his window, puffed out his lips. "Wave to her," he said.

"I am, of course."

"I wish you weren't leaving now," he added.

"You mean because of Mom?"

"Yes," his father said—and waved a final time. "She's not saying anything, but she's depended on you."

"What for?"

They turned the corner. The view of the house was gone.

"It's hard to explain," his father answered, frowning toward the evening road. "There are some things I think—there are some things I think I don't understand about her. She had this promise, of course, this musical promise."

"You mean as a pianist?"

"Yes, of course."

"I know she liked to play, but I didn't know she had more than that."

"She had—she wanted—much more than that."

"What happened?"

"What do you mean, 'what happened'? We got married. We were living in San Francisco at the time." His father's tone had become angry, defensive, suddenly, and he hesitated as if to ward it off. They were crossing the Jutland bridge, which was covered, now, with the coppery green of rust and the orange enamelling of the sun. "Your mother," he went on, "was dragging me to one concert after another, and then there was your Aunt Shirley, who came along too and was driving me crazy with her Shakespearean hysterics —just like your Aunt Ellen's. But worse. I remember going one time to Maurice Evans in *Hamlet*—who was the toast of San Francisco—and she kept repeating that phrase of his—I remember it—'but, break, my heart, for I must hold my tongue.'—she, your Aunt Shirley, if you can imagine, was trying to imitate Maurice Evans. Finally I said, 'But, I'll break your jaw, if you don't hold your tongue.' Your mother never forgave me."

Ed laughed. "Shutting Aunt Shirley up is something you dream about."

"Well," his father said wryly. "I dreamed about it, all right. It became a nightmare, because your mother thought I had mortally wounded her sister. They both thought I was the most uncouth person on earth. Anyway, after that, I stopped going to concerts. And your mother dwindled off in her degree at Berkeley, which was quickly becoming Red in those days, and I said, 'I've got a new territory—the Northwest. Are you coming with me or not?' And she came." He paused, while he turned into the intersection and then on—along Elliott Bay Boulevard and then finally into the waterfront streets of downtown Seattle. The seafood stands and restaurants were just being lit, the neon fish sending up flaring blue bubbles beside the Seven-Up bottling plant, whose tower presented, still, a capped green diver flying off within a perfect emerald globe. "But what I meant to say was," his father continued, "I'm not so sure all of that was right. Your mother leaving Berkeley especially."

"Why do you feel that way now?" Ed asked.

"It's more complicated," his father said. "But as I was saying, I think it's hard for your mother that you're leaving. You've filled in where I couldn't."

The admission surprised Ed, kept him silent.

"I tried being interested in those things—in her concerts, her plays—but it just never did work out. I've always been," he said, putting on one of his guises, "a pretty crude so-and-so, with only a high-school education."

Ed, angered by the guise, said, "But you feel different now—you said so—about Mom. So you must feel different about yourself."

"About myself? No, I can't say that. But what I meant was—we used to be able to see things more clearly. I used to say, 'Well, now, Berkeley's Red and you—your mother—should get out of there.' But now, there's Vietnam, and you could be sent there, and I don't know what to say. And then that has this effect where maybe I should have let your mother stay where she was."

He had pulled up for a brief stop at his downtown office in the Wymansales Building; he was gone in an instant, would return in an instant, and Ed, alone in the idling car, was left to stare through the gilt-lettered glass doors, up one half flight into the long back lobby, past the red light globes and along the fading walls and floors carpeted with grey evening light. He wondered if his father would return just as confessional, or if this was a way of drawing a line across the conversation, of starting out fresh again.

On the opposite side of the street, the abandoned Atlas Theater stood with its topmost cornices shining with the high-water marks of the sun—now at its sharpest angle—the central emblem raising great, briefly golden muscles as it shouldered the entire earth. "When I get to school," Ed said to himself, "I will begin with second quarter Latin." In the night darkness of the Park-and-Lock eight stories below, the safety light went on above the collection box, brightening the posters on the northern wall of the theater: "An Evening with Shakespeare—Consisting of a Series of Recitations of the Bard's Most Beloved Speeches." The poster hung islanded above the backdoor with the $10,000 threat if entered, the passageway dividing, so that one could cross down into the adjoining Atlas Pool. What a collection the Atlas block must have been—a theater, a pool, a hotel, a restaurant, and a cleaners. His mother had taken him there once—to a pool which had seemed nothing more than a condemned flooded underground, with columns rising from four corners, tentatively supporting a ceiling corniced with ill-tempered snapping bass, overarching swimmers who sometimes ran right into the columns when the instructors weren't looking.

His father returned. "Just had to get this order book," he said. "We were fresh out at home. And Webb might want to order something."

Ed didn't answer, only looked at the green, four-carboned tablet, which he had seen countless times before—at the engraved tree—and wondered why his father was fooling himself. He knew that Webb would never buy shoes from him again, just as surely as he knew that once they arrived at Stanford, he wouldn't be able to work.

"I see you brought the memoirs," his father said, moving the car into the brief traffic once again and patting the books between them. "Any special reason?"

"I just wanted to find out more about Grandfather."

"I can tell you all you need to know."

"You idealize him," Ed said.

His father looked over. "I do?"

"Yes. I can remember when I was about four—he wasn't so sweet-tempered. I used to turn the light off on him in the bathroom, and he'd come out all lathered and mad holding his long razor and strap."

"Well, your memory may be a little slanted. At four years? Actually, Father was very mild, very cultured. He taught school—including high school—and back in those days those higher grades were just like college. And then he had that farm that he lived on and worked as a side venture."

"Yes, but—"

"He was a man perfectly at ease with himself. I can remember a time after we had moved back into St. Louis, and he came home looking like he'd been through the mill—or more so than usual—and Mother said to him, 'Dad, it's not worth it—we can try the school again.' And he said, 'No, Mother, no, today a man came in with a vat he'd used for gasoline and he wanted one of our men to weld it, and I said, No, too dangerous, might explode. And do you know what happened? The man went straight down the block and got another outfit to do it and the whole thing exploded and killed two men. I've got to stay on,' he said, 'because there isn't anyone else around to do honest business.' "

"I know—but why is everything so gloomy in his memoirs after he left his school and farm and went to St. Louis?"

His father hedged. "He didn't have as much time for his books, of course. And he didn't have his farm."

"I don't mean that. It just seems like the last pages are bitter."

"Why are you asking this now?"

"One of the reasons I brought the memoirs," Ed admitted, "is that I thought I could carry on a family legacy."

"Legacy?'

"Yes, I know Granddad always wanted to go to college—and Mom always wanted to finish."

"So you think you're doing it for them," his father said, angry. "What a stupid idea."

Ed, silent and furious with himself for having revealed his secret, looked wildly about for some refuge. But the last had been taken. He wished he had taken time that morning to drive down to their church and receive Communion. Perhaps then he could have been stronger. Sitting and praying in the pew, he could easily imagine himself kneeling beneath the pressure of Christ's hands, and could even imagine himself being lifted to the head of God, which hung in his spherical and childlike universe like a triangular fresco cornered in the Sistine Chapel. Why had he lost this perfect opportunity for gaining strength?

His father looked at him again and said—as if with conciliation—"Yes, I'll have to admit Dad was bitter. It goes back to what I was saying about Mom."

"Yes?" He was too wounded to speak further.

"I only meant to say that Father and your mother got along famously after he came to live with us. When I would come home from work he would only set me off."

"But wasn't that because they were both interested in the same things?"

"If you mean culture—yes, partly. When we had that Zenith with the compass dial before you were born, we used to listen to the Voice of Firestone. When I was subjected to that every Thursday night or whenever it was, I used to think of hell coming right into my own living room. And then later when we had TV for the short time that Father was alive, it was Playhouse 90, when they had those dozens and dozens of empty pregnant pauses, when the prompter was probably going nuts just off stage—waving 1500 different idiot boards at them all at once, and never getting them to look."

"I never heard this before," Ed said. "The way I always understood it—you and Grandfather always got on perfectly."

"Too perfectly," his father said.

They came to the Seattle Tunnel and were silent in the sudden darkness and scattered electric light which led them, finally, out onto the Floating Bridge. On the water, the wind was catching the meticulously cut sails of the night-cruising craft, their lights like fragments of jewels thrown on the huge lake, or into the sky. Almost immediately the city was gone; they were passing the brief neon of the East Gate—the blue crosses of the veterinary clinics and way-station county hospitals—and then the mountains reclaimed them totally. The route wound past the foot of a scarcely outlined Mount Si—a row of heavily berried mountain ash—into North Bend and then they were up over Snoqualmie Pass, and then down again, catching glimpses of the huge incinerators of the sawdust towns, their smoke heavy with cascading cinders, bright as fireworks. At Cle Elum, they made a stop at a late-night dimestore, where a child drew pictures lazily on the condensation of the front window, and they were out again and down the side of the mountain, where they saw, in the partial light, the forests of evergreen dwindle into sagebrush. On the outskirts of Eurkay the land dried and flattened suddenly, and in the wash of stars and moon, low-depth rivers passed through a country that was a transition, looking back to the Cascades while beginning the endless flats of the Columbia Basin.

"Why, Mr. Hill—Ed," Mrs. Webb said at the door to the farmhouse. "Sam isn't here. He's up in the mountains fishing."

And so Ed was placed in the spare room until their search for Webb could continue in the morning (his father insisted). And Ed, tense and fatigued, took out his sketchbooks —poetry and drawings—and set them beside his grandfather's memoirs, while he pulled back the curtains, revealing a clear sky, the crystalline dipper. Lying on the bed, he could sometimes hear what seemed to be the flutterings of hands through cabinets and drawers—as if Mrs. Webb were still straightening things, in a dream. And just outside the window, on the Webbs' great vista of acreage, the aspen trees twinkled like four vertical brooks, skimming coin-shaped leaves across the pond. On the other side of the grove, there were the other sounds, muted, half-formed, but distinctly human. One voice would rise up, then descend; another would rise up, descend—like flights of meteors answering each other. From the hill came a scarcely distinguishable, half-rosette glow, as if, in the next grove over, dozens upon dozens of torches were being lit.

He eased down into near-sleep, and as he did, the Big Dipper folded and collapsed, noiselessly. The aspens skimmed metallic leaves which bounced from pond to sky, becoming meteors. And as the constellations moved, they pulled at the great drapery of dark, revealing a dawn at the outer border. As he slept, Ed felt himself breathe to the rhythms of Communion and the incantations from behind the hills.

THREE

"To Edward Garrett Hill, My Grandson and Namesake, These Memoirs Are Lovingly Inscribed.

"I have been almost everywhere, but my boyhood and early adolescence, save for one extremely important disturbance, were spent in southern Illinois, out in the land of the Methodist 'Meeting House,' out in the land of Marion Chapel, where passion and austerity, discipline and freedom, joined together. I remember that Marion Chapel was a severely plain structure, about thirty by forty feet in dimensions, without belfry or porches, or other exterior ornaments, and was seldom well-painted. Its wide, staring windows were without blinds or curtains, and the lawn was unrelieved by any trees, shrubs or flowers. Its interior was as plain and poor as the exterior. Two plain front doors opened to two aisles, flanked by hard oak seats, made by local carpenters.

"The Presiding Elder was nearly always in attendance, and preached the sermon, and with the Circuit Rider assisting, he administered the Holy Sacrament of the Lord's Supper. I shall never forget the deep solemnity of the moments when he read the 'Confession': 'We have sinned by thought, word, and deed, provoking most justly Thy wrath and indignation against us'—'Have mercy upon us, most Merciful Father'—and then the 'Invitation'—'Ye that do truly and earnestly repent you of your sins, and are in love and charity with your neighbors, and intend to lead a new life, following the commandments of God, and walking henceforth in His holy ways, draw near with faith, take this cup, devoutly kneeling.' Most of the people responded reverently, while the

Minister, with intense solemnity, repeated, 'The blood of our Lord Jesus Christ, which was shed for you.'

"When we arose, it was with downcast eyes, and then, suddenly, all the Chapel seemed to change. Sitting on the hard oak seat, I began to envision how the pioneer carpenter must have raised that building; the high beams stretched before me, strong, shapely, beautiful. Immediately I could hear some kind of grand music, rising up once, up again, lifting, lifting the rafters, forming a vault. And then a great slant of light was crossing the Chapel, and I was rushing out-of-doors, trying not to be too hurried.

"To the east, and south, and westward from our home were interspersed rolling tracts of prairie and timber lands —the farms and houses of the pioneers. Beginning with our home, an almost level prairie—with scarcely a tree visible on the landscape—stretched in an unbroken plane to the Embarras River, about twenty-five miles to the northward, where lay a heavily timbered belt of land along the river bottoms. Continuing past this, another prairie stretched almost endlessly, for nearly two hundred miles, terminating in clouds. I stood watching. The springing grass seemed to greet me with a smile, and the dewdrops, pendant from the tips of the grass blades, and shimmering as they refracted the rainbow colors, seemed to confide, joyously, 'This is God's world, made for the happiness of children.' I ran through the grass, through the underbrush, discovering some sparrow's eggs that were speckled, beautiful. It seemed like an expression of trust and peace. And over the fields and pathways, the meadow lark soared and sang, and from fence rows by the roadside, and from solitary places on the remoter prairie, the wild rose peered in shy beauty.

"All of this occurred in 1872. In the spring of 1873, the disruption was to occur which—although it was later to be covered over—was to have the greatest and most sustained effect upon my young life. In that spring, my father and uncle bought a large tract of timber and farm land on Raccoon Creek, in Owen County, Indiana, wherein could be found a lake and excellent watermill. We made our move from Pleasant View, Illinois—in covered wagons, driving our milkcows ahead of us.

"The trip was a thrilling one for a boy in his tenth year, and I remember it distinctly yet. After passing woodland streams and newly settled prairies, we went through Robinson, the county seat of Crawford County, Illinois, and from there on, we had a fine prairie view of the country which sloped gradually to the big Wabash River. On the Indiana side of the river were high precipitous bluffs with the town of Merom atop one of the bluffs, crowned with a beautiful college building, a structure of fine architectural proportions.

"We first caught sight of the college building when we were about fifteen miles away, but we were not aware of the purpose of this growing mirage until we reached the town.

"We crossed the Wabash on small ferryboats, and with much effort, made the way up to the bluff, toward the town. How could I have known that I had already decided to attend the college? We passed the resonant archways, their stately buttresses crossed and recrossed by great insignias of learning, and then we moved on, slowly into town.

"It was then that the change arrived. While the others were occupied, I stole quietly away and hurried back to look at the magnificent architectural proportions and then, on to the bluff's edge, to look back over the prairie county in Illinois, over which we had just come. (To this day, I always see this college, these precipitous cliffs, whenever I open my collected works of Eliot, Fielding, Dickens, or Shakespeare—whose frontispieces contain for me the figures I saw embroidered on the walls of the college.)

"How long I remained there, I do not know, but I was finally aroused by my father, who had been alarmed by my disappearance and provoked over the delay I had caused the whole caravan. He brought me to attention with a jerk and after telling me of his fright, said that if he had known the facts, he would have gone on without me.

"From that time forward, I carried a mental image of the college with me, and through the entire period of our settling in our new home, and even through the failure of the crops, and our subsequent return back to Pleasant View, I carried the decision that I would find a way of pursuing a course of study.

"The decision was made silently, and it may be difficult to believe that I had resolved to keep my secret from my father until the evening of my high-school graduation. I remember that I had given the valedictory oration of 'Rocks and Pilots,' with the theme, 'All things must cease,' and that after the ceremony, all of us went over to the home of my friend, Frank Chapman, who had graduated also. Our fathers were good friends, and there was also the tie between our grandfathers. I remember being struck, as I had been that whole afternoon, by the greatness of Frank's closing oration, 'The Fifth Act.' What it was about it is hard to name; the best I can say is that he took his idea from Shakespeare and then through turns of a quiet rhetoric, led us back to where we were, back to farms and church meetings. He had looked so fragile while taking his place upon the platform and yet, then, so strong, when the finely chiseled piece began to form before our eyes.

"In the evening, Frank went into his room to change out of his Sunday clothes while the rest of the men went outside for a walk. I remember coming down from the second floor and seeing the men out in the fields, talking. There was such a quiet in the orchards, and the mown fields stretched out in plane after plane. Single clouds hung in the sky like lone bundles of golden hay, and the sunset had changed the living room windows into what seemed to me to be oil paintings, oil paintings of waves at twilight—all russet, pink, pearl. And still the men were talking.

"It was then—as I stood at the window and watched my father kneel down and scoop something out of the soil—that I began to understand those things which had kept my father alive: waking up at dawn and opening the windows, the air as cold as a splash of pond water; ploughing in even rows and watching the blade rub clean against the soil; lifting the leaf of a vine you thought would die and finding something living there; standing at your living room window and listening to the sunflower stalks crack in the evening heat; stepping out into the corn patch and, for apparently no reason at all, moving your hand through the earth. It was all this and more—it was not definable. It had to do with the orchards, the fields, the harvesting, with the way all of these things interrelated with the house itself. What my father took in, through the very air he breathed, was some great architectonic sense of the way the fields gave life to the house, a sense not so very distant from that childhood experience of mine, that experience of a Sunday, 1872. So how could I ask him about college? I wanted to stay with him. Stay with him! And continue in that widening interchange of houses and fields.

"And so in the autumn I went to teach school in Pleasant View, having given up my distant goal of college. In the late afternoons I would return to work in the fields, my innermost self veritably hurting with the pleasure of balances: the mental warfare of teaching the children Latin and geography, and the swaying muscular tension of delving the spade into the soil.

"After my father passed on and I subsequently married—relatively late in life—the school work still continued, and I even managed to work on a primer for school-aged children, on several levels, while still sustaining the life of the farm. But the demands, in the wake of my father's death, were inestimable. One year would be fair (under him it would have been good to superior), and the next year would bring a shock from which there was no recovery. My evening reading ceased. I arose at four, went to bed at midnight, in hopes of keeping the legacy. And all the while the regret was growing, surrounding the vision of the college I had dismissed. I gave up the teaching position, and with the aid of my wife and three children—who were now of age—tried holding on. But my techniques had become blunted during my country squire's repose.

"In 1920—presumably the year when times were beginning to turn for others—we lost everything. I packed whatever items could be salvaged, and with my family traveled by auto to Saint Louis. We had nothing, but I managed to be hired on in the farm machinery business. I became a salesman.

"For years I wondered if my visions of the college had been colored by my imagination as a child. Then finally in the course of my business, I came to Merom, in an auto, from the Indiana side of the town. It was late of a Saturday, and there was a renewed quiet as before, surrounding the cliffs. A blanket of sunlight rested on top of the archways, creating cellars of shadow below, in a picture which presented the college in exact halves, with the sunset city above, and the foundation of blackness below, bringing me to remember that night of slow-moving ferrying and the circle of our caravan fires.

". . . And now I must provide this ellipsis because a great amount of time has elapsed since these memoirs were first conceived. They have not grown as one might expect: they have been transcribed again and again, with individual words added and deleted, with snippets or fragments pieced together.

"My name is Edward Beecher Hill. I am living in the home of my son, Tom R. Hill, and my daughter-in-law, Karin Hill. I write with a pencil, because I can't handle a pen, successfully, anymore. This notebook was purchased in Seattle, Washington. During the recording of the above memoir, I had a hold of a syntactical skill which I no longer possess. I could fit sentences together, create the sounds and positions I wanted. It is very bitter to me that I cannot regain this skill. I just celebrated my 88th birthday on October 30th. The War between the States was in full blast when I was born. My people were Virginians, originally. They sang war songs, such as 'Marching through Georgia,' 'John

Brown's body lies mouldering in the tomb,' and others. We sang, 'Hurrah! Hurrah! We bring the jubilee! Hurrah! Hurrah! The flag that makes you free!' and other patriotic songs. One church song which I well remember my father singing was, 'I will arise and go to Jesus, he will embrace me in his arms. In the arms of my dear Saviour, Oh! there are ten thousand charms!' The hymn books contain much fine poetry, I think."

To find Webb, they had to backtrack forty miles—back up into the Cascades. Mrs. Webb had said he was at Lake Goheen, staying either at the resort or at the "estate" of Mr. Collier, on the far western shore.

They turned off onto an old logging road. Within moments, the lake was visible through the trees like spaces of blue sky.

"This Collier," Ed said. "I think he's the one I used to work for back in Seattle."

"You did?"

"Yes—on the *Jutland News* before we moved out to Windsor."

"The throwaway?"

"Yes, and you didn't want me to work for him—neither you nor Mom, because he was an avowed atheist."

"Yes, I do remember him; he was always editorializing everyone into the ground, but I don't see how it could be him."

Ed could tell his father had not slept. His gestures were fragmented, the shakiness distinct from the continual jarring of the road. The attentive determination of the previous afternoon still remained, but Ed could see that as Webb eluded them more and more on increasingly narrow roads, his father was being led toward a deep tension which it would not be possible to break. And there would be no convenient oblivion.

"Dad—look at that lily pond! Those are the hugest flowers I've ever seen."

"Yes, they are beautiful. When we get to the resort, we'll try and find Webb, and then we'll take a little time out and go fishing. All right with you? I haven't been here for years."

"Don't you think we ought to get back on the road, soon as we can?"

"Plenty of time, plenty of time"—with his face still shaking while they moved along the rutted road.

The resort office and random cabins came into view, like a blurry snapshot: raw logs and shingles, a central bathhouse, and a Coca-Cola sign to distinguish the main building from the others. "I'm looking for Sam Webb," his father said to the proprietor once they were inside. The wind, chilled and clean from the lake, ballooned in through the windows.

"He just left," the proprietor said. "He's down at the dock in Collier's boat."

And outside once more, they were flagging down a man in a russet skiff. The wind was all around them, the air so clean that the dust could be tasted.

"I have to talk to you," his father shouted to the man.

Webb cupped his ear, feigned ignorance for a moment, and then signalled them to jump on.

The jump was instantaneous: the boat had circled back close to the dock; Ed leaped across the few inches of opaque water, with his father close behind.

"Hold on until we get out of this wind."

Ed gripped the side, while instinctively the three formed a balance.

"Webb, turn down that motor!" his father shouted.

But he went unheard. Webb drove the boat ruthlessly across the lake, the waves whitecapping against the sides and spraying them from all directions. Ed looked up for a moment and saw the sun darken in an instant, throwing an avalanche of shadow across the lakeside mountain. As if startled, an eagle came out of a grove of pines that was as smooth and even as mown, rain-drenched grass; the wings, in shadow, preceded them into miniscule horse latitudes, where Webb finally slowed the boat.

"Quite a ride and quite a motor," Webb said, shifting into neutral. "I just wanted to give you the feel of it. It's Collier's."

"You know I've been trying to get a hold of you. Why didn't you answer my letter?" his father asked.

Ed was certain Webb didn't perceive his tension until now. It seemed to strengthen him. And supply tact. "How could I do that, Tom? I didn't know what to say. You know I'm all washed up with the Company."

"Know it? Know it?" His father made a sudden movement and set the boat rocking. "Turn that goddamn motor off and listen to me." The idling motor stopped. There was a huge rush of wind across the mountain, even while the lake was still. "What I need to know is, did you do anything to provoke the Company into taking that loan away from you?"

Ed looked at Webb—could see strokes and heart attacks in his face. "Other than some bad seasons—no. But what difference does it make, Tom? It's all over and done with."

Even though Webb was becoming aware of his gaze, Ed could not look away. As the skiff moved up and down in the easy, scarcely audible waves, he began to feel Webb becoming like the countless playmates he had known as a child—the children, the boys, the men, who, despite or because of their handicaps, always gain sway.

"No, it isn't all over and done with," his father answered —and now Ed could predict it—"because if you're not in the wrong, I'm going to go to St. Louis and defend you. Have it out with Foley."

Webb raised his brows, which were accentuated by the re-emerging sun. "You can't do that."

"Why not?"

"Because you and I both know"—nodding, for some reason, toward Ed—"what will happen."

"What?"

And then, as if in deference to Ed, Webb hesitated.

"They'll fire you. Maybe Foley won't do it directly, but they will. They've got all of our numbers—do I have to say this? —I'm a West Green retailer just as sure as you're a West Green salesman. They're going to call all the old lines in and name everything Consolidated, which means phasing us out."

Although his father had said as much himself, Ed could see that he was humiliated by the facts—as they came from an outsider at the steering wheel. And Webb, as he had spoken, had seemed to be strengthened even further; the sound of his own voice had made the ultimate difference in the balance. And so he could afford to be generous. "And now that we've gotten that out of the way, let's make you take some time off, at least for a couple hours. I saw you there on the dock and I said, 'By Golly, I'm going to get him to do a little fishing.' How long has it been since you've fished?"

"Two years maybe," his father said, tense, distracted.

"Well, let's set ourselves out in the middle of the lake before we beach it and do some trolling, and then when we're done with that, I want you to meet Collier down at the end. That's where I'm staying."

The small talk covered them over like a second wing of shadow—Stanford, the War—Webb had two sons in Vietnam—but Ed was aware that even as his father fished, he was working out his strategy, his new plan of rectitude. He knew, now, why his father had brought them here, even to an obscure lake fed by snows like a lap of water in the Cascades; he wanted to find out if Webb was worth it. And he had decided, yes, he was. And that was why Ed kept staring at the man—how could he possibly equal the value of his father? Or be worth any of his greatest efforts?

He was distracted by some colors. "There's my caboose," Webb said, pointing. "Would you believe that they tossed it this far?"

On the southern shore, perhaps three miles from the dock of the resort, Ed could see a train car lying on its side, amid some crushed trees. CHOW-DOWN CABOOSE was written below the windows, one color per word, with different teeth in the letters cracked or missing. Its top was split down the center, and the panes were spider-webbed by a B-B gun.

"That was a diner I had when I was about your age," Webb went on, looking at him.

"I thought you always had the store," Ed said.

"No—and things even went fine the first year. Then the coal went bad up in Cle Elum, and I had to close. Marlice was pregnant then. Lousy."

"And then weren't you taking care of your parents?" his father asked.

"Yes. It was then—" looking at Ed once more, "—that your father came along and bailed me out. Helped me get a loan." He turned around, so as to escape the original view. "It was a fresh start."

"But how did the caboose get all the way out here?" his father asked.

"Marlice heard that the people got to thinking it was an eyesore near town, so they simply tossed it in the wilderness. She was furious when she heard about it, she'd held onto it in her mind."

Ed, watching his pole dip among the even grooves of sun, thought of the morning, with Marlice Webb getting breakfast, while all the windows poured in the threat of rain. Away from the house—and between the hills—the field of corn had been darkening under thunderheads; and further on, greying sycamores had stood out against a backdrop of sky that was the color of olive leaves. Inside, the house had been full of the shadows of curtains that fluttered like spooked fish, with Mrs. Webb saying, "Ed, reach down in that second drawer and get that packet I've been fixing for your mother," and with Ed, pocketing the relics, still seeing the woman when she had answered his father's knock—the night before; she had stood hesitating behind the leaded glass oval, dressed in a green, old-fashioned dress which the glass divided into the ribbons of willows, and when she had finally opened the door, she had seemed the exact replica of the 1930's matron who posed in a loose gown on the piano easel. "Ed, your father said you must call your draft board before you leave. Don't worry about the long distance. It's past eight, they'll be open." "There it is again," Ed had said, nearly audibly. "That persistence. Why do they want me in Vietnam?" He had taken up the receiver and found the needed information: "Full-time study is 15 credits under a quarter system. If you drop a course, your college is obliged to report the change, which could immediately qualify you for I-A."

His father's pole formed an arc, nearly touching the water, and he reeled in. Automatically, without enjoyment, he put the trout, lashing, in the basket. Webb, apparently sensing the deadness, said, "Hey—we're almost to Collier's now. Let's reel in, and we'll talk him into giving us some lunch."

"Webb," his father broke in, as if emerging from a daze, "what will you do if you lose the store?"

Webb stopped reeling. "Easy—just farm."

"But you only get vegetables off that. That isn't enough to keep you going."

"I'll just add on. Besides, I've got backing.

"Who from?"

"Every relative in the county."

Ed could now hear the waterfall where Collier's place was reported to be; Webb merely had to throw the boat in gear for a few seconds, and then they could see the formation of a chalet cabin, with a rough stone chimney formidably squared against the pines. A county fair garden of mixed flowers and vegetables rolled down to the water, nearly touching the dock, where they tied the boat. In a moment, Ed found himself walking into a gentleman's living room. On the other side of the house, there was a decided repetition of a hammer, above the cascading of the waterfall, still hidden. The hammer continued even through Webb's making of the coffee, so that when Collier emerged, Ed felt he had been surprised in the midst of housebreaking.

Beside Webb, Collier seemed an ampler, more massive

version of the short-statured man; he appeared more heavily set in his strength. There was a crisp music to his talk, and Ed could remember how he would often wait around Collier's newspaper backshop just to hear him yell out, "page two," when the typeset was ready. His hands would move him on to page three, and he would always mentally reorder the columns first by squaring his eye. Then when the page was finally prepared, he would roll out the ink and then form a sample page by sheeting the paper and malleting down on a cushioning block. Ed, thinking of the Jonsonian tribute to Shakespeare, saw Collier as striking his own energies upon an anvil, giving them shape, direction; and if they didn't work the first time, he would give them a second heat. There seemed, in fact, to be a kind of Jonsonian resonance in his voice—a voice which demanded craft and projected it in his acutely made poems—artifacts of a carefully wrought heritage. "Your lines are too unsure," he had said to Ed when he had grown old enough to entrust them, "your illustrations are as leaky as your sonnets. Remember that sonnets have to be pretty rooms."

"So you're Mr. Hill," Collier said.

"Sorry we just helped ourselves to everything," his father said, shaking hands, and looking very pale in his clasp.

"No problem. Webb told me everything. I'm sorry to see that you're fretted away with worry."

"Not exactly that," his father said in defense.

"And here," Collier went on, "is your son the budding poet and illustrator. Or is it architecture now? How's your work coming? Are you going to get the education you need for it?"

"Yes," his father said, "in fact I'm just in the midst of taking him to Stanford."

"Well, maybe they'll teach you there and maybe they won't," Collier said, sitting down.

"What do you mean?" his father asked, angry and tense again.

"See all of this"—pointing to his library—"I built all of

this myself. Never had a full day's education beyond high school. But I still do my reading, post my poems once a week, and get my letters in at the *Eurkay Star.* I've been knocked about quite a bit, but I don't mind saying I just got my honorary doctorate from Central Northwest last year."

"Yes, I've lived through all of that, too," his father said. "All that crap about the school of hard knocks. And I know enough about it to save my 1500 dollars to match my son's 1500 dollars—a good part of it by the way was his paper route money—so he could at least have a good first year at an excellent school."

"And look where it's gotten you—you now have a large packet of worry."

"If you call working for my family—right"—and then he added—"in the eyes of God—if you call all that a packet of worry, then it's something I should be thankful for."

"There you are," Collier said, seemingly delighted with the turn, "you've interposed God between your work and you."

"And why not?" Ed said, startling them by speaking up. "That's where your sense of rightness comes from."

"Oh my God what garbage," Webb said, laughing. "If He's around, why is the Company firing the hell out of our rightness?"

"And it's your conception of God," Collier went on, looking at Ed and stunning him with his memory, "that's responsible for all that flimsy Renaissance architecture in your poems—and sketches."

"I'm not going to sit here and have my son insulted," his father said, standing up. "Not my son—or me."

"Sit down, sit down," Webb said. "Collier's like this with everyone. He likes to get people's dander up, so they'll say things for his writing. See how fast he got you talking—like philosophers."

"Like hell," Collier said. "It's just that I see Hill sitting here with a crucifixion in his face, and I've decided to point out some alternatives to him."

"You have no alternatives," his father said. "Except the one you're living in right now. I don't know how I got on this topic—but look at you. You've got no home, no family. You've pulled yourself up by the roots—"

"And deliberately, deliberately," Collier broke in. "I couldn't stand neighborhoods anymore—like the kind you and I lived in—"

"And now here you are easily preaching separation."

"I'm only saying," Collier insisted, "that you've got a door open in front of you—why not walk right through it instead of beating your head against a wall?"

"That's pretty general advice," his father said.

"Dad, let's go." Ed was standing up.

"Then, I'll make it specific," Webb said. "Quit the Company."

"You're a goddamn fool," Ed said and walked out.

Outside, he followed the outlet of the waterfall to its source, past screens of birch and fern, which fanned in the wind, imitating the sound of water. Jumping between polished stones, he could hear the roar moving in toward him. With lessening energy, the water followed a wider and wider course and then, suddenly, opened into a pool. Rising above the water was a cliff of sage-colored stone, over which the cascade fell, widening into stillness. Jet after jet fell, like the paths of ever-descending silver fish. One fish would leap from the precipice, fall, and—and Ed would like to have said, "dive," dive into the pool, but immediately his eye was taken up to the top of the precipice again, and another fish was leaping, falling, its path finding no terminus but in the origin of the next descending spray.

Immediately he was out of his clothes and diving into the pool. Fragments of afternoon sun glittered in front of him like nautical fireflies. His father was a fool to stand by Webb. He dove again. And he knew Collier was false—could prove that he was.

He got out and, naked, sat on a log. He felt—free—of every bit of worry. He was free, a god on a rock, flexing his muscles, and diving again. When he rose from the water, his father was coming up the path.

"I saw you from the beach," he called above the water. "I brought you a towel."

"Thanks," Ed said, holding out a hand. But he felt shy of his father's eyes and became conscious of his own whiteness. And yet even in the midst of withdrawing, he wished, desperately, that his father would take the towel and dry him off—as he had when he was a child. Chilled, he put on his underclothes, hoping his father was not looking. For a moment, a locust came out, piercing the roar of the cascade, but he was closed to it.

"I don't think Webb's insulted," his father said, "when you left we all said some things to smooth it all over."

Reddening, Ed put on the rest of his clothes and headed down the path. When they got to the boat, he said, "And you're worried if Webb's insulted? I think you're as much a fool to defend him as he thinks you are."

His father turned on him. "You have no idea what he represents, do you?" he said.

"No," Ed answered, "especially after seeing him."

And then Webb emerged, to ferry them back.

FOUR

They did not spend a second night at Mrs. Webb's but drove out straight after dinner. And suddenly there was nothing but grass, hills, and a radio tower: red beacon, red beacon. They passed a railroad station and then the Purina signs. The constellations came out, arching spines of stars; then the road brought them to a park, loud with crickets.

In the silence of the car, Ed pictured the Webb's garden, their house, and in it, he was moving from cellar to attic—tripping on the unlit stairs, bumping against doors and tables; his hands were moving across desks, chairs, drawers, stacks of papers, rods and reels, old photographs, Classic comic books, folders of old poems, the packet prepared for his mother. And then he was standing at the bedroom window, looking at the image—his father—as it moved through the cabbage patch, bending at each plant. The stretch of earth beneath his father's feet extended into the back fields, into the darkening windbreak. Once or twice, a car would flash out from the roads, which were invisible, now, upon the high-rocked night mountains, as the sun's searchlights of rose moved toward islanded clouds, focusing as they lengthened.

But now, in the car, as his father sat perfectly rigid, breaking his solitude, Ed could instantly feel the formation of a voice at the back of his mind, the critic which Collier had conjured. It was railing against him, guessing at his father's accusing silence; it seemed to have been there for an indeterminate amount of time—like an unnoticed ringing in his ears. "Did you ever want to farm?" Ed asked.

"Farm? I did farm with your grandfather. In fact, when I was about your age, I farmed and had my own dairy."

"I know—but I mean now."

His father observed him—critically—once again. "I hadn't really thought about it."

"I was just thinking how great it would be if we could just stay on at the Webbs'—except it would be our farm. And then we could be on our own. Self-sufficient."

His father laughed bitterly. Even so, Ed knew it was not meant for him. "That would be a tradition! 'This is God's world made for the happiness of children.' That's the way my father used to talk about our farm, with his father helping him. Oh my God how beautiful it was supposed to be. He used to have that touch, he used to say, where he could feel if his mental and physical balances were evening themselves out during the day. He used to say, 'And if I felt like they weren't, my father would shoulder a little more of the physical, and I'd shoulder a little more of the mental.' Oh my God what an idealist. Well, I guess plants and animals had voices and gestures for him and his father, but they didn't for me."

"That's what I was asking about earlier—about the way Grandfather felt—"

"He thought," his father went on, not listening, "that he was a failure for being a salesman, so why shouldn't I be one too? All I can remember in the final years of that farm we had near Pleasant View was Dad holding onto that piece of family property like it was his life raft in the ocean, or the last copy of Shakespeare or the Bible after the atomic blast. Can you understand that, Ed? The farm had failed five years prior, and here he was, a naive scholarly fool still pretending to live among his 'balances.' Balances? Christ, if he was anything he was the most imbalanced man I ever knew: working my mother into her grave, worrying my sister because she was the eldest, and asking *me* to start a dairy because he needed some 'subordinate' income. He had the gall to call it 'subordinate.' And so I had to scrape through high school and do double-time once I graduated just to help him make ends meet through his ridiculous dream—just because he idealized what he had with his father.'

"How could you—"

"And then in the spring," his father said, still refusing to listen, "in the spring of our last year, the river was swollen from the rains and busted the dam into a million pieces. And what happened? Our farm was swamped, my father of course went bankrupt, and yet out of moral uprightness, he wanted us to slave to pay back the money he owed. I said to him, 'I wouldn't throw one more red cent down that mudhole of a farm.' After that he became a salesman and shut up. And after that my sister—Aunt Ann—always claims he had a chronic nervous breakdown." His father, spent, looked out over the night road. "That's why I'm looking forward to you doing something at school. This cycle's got to break somewhere."

"I'm not sure I'll do any better than Grandfather."

"Of course you will. We're all depending on you."

And Ed's voice—still at the back of his mind—told him that his father was looking for two kinds of support, neither of which he could offer. He wanted to know that his son backed his decision and understood it—and that he would have the confidence to fulfill the prophecy which, Ed now had to admit, had originally been his own—to carry the memoirs forward.

Through the night—they stayed on the Oregon border—the voice followed him, so that when they were on the road again, he felt pressed in a different direction.

"Suppose," he said, "I should get the idea that I'm a Conscientious Objector—while I'm at school. Would you have a look at it—I'd send you a copy—and tell me what you think?"

"A copy of what?"

"You have to make a statement," Ed said. "One that's theologically precise."

His father looked upset—but in another way. "You're not

talking about changing anything, are you? Anything to do with your first year at Stanford?"

"No, but the statement should be made and filed no matter what your deferments happen to be."

"I don't want," his father said, tapping the steering wheel, "any disruptions as far as our investment is concerned. It's too important to me right now. Don't think about C.O. until they try to nail you, and if I understand right, that won't happen for another four years."

The evergreens were now completely gone—that morning they had abandoned a motel that had been a steep-pitched mountain inn of pineboard and multi-colored lights hung along the eaves—but now they were moving through a mauve country of thin birds and cedar. In a moment they would take a wrong turn and wind, eventually, to the top of Crater Lake, whose blue depth would seem to reach, unspeakably, all the way to a sea on the opposite side of the earth and reflect, even so, the Russian sky beneath, fraught with stars and iridescent fish. And Ed would say—in answer to the voice—"I can come up with a plan that is theologically sound. I can register my belief as a Conscientious Objector and still be a legitimate student. And I can write and draw poems and configurations that are precise."

On the correct road again, they would pass the Elizabethan theater of the Oregon coast, and Ed would write, "Saw my first fall colors today, tucked below in some shade —wildly red vine maple. The car's shadow was ahead of us at the time. Fall has gone up in flames." And the sunset country would change again; trees would rise up once more as if to prologue the night—with the redwoods emerging—and they would wind around the lower cliffs, until the fog, the ghost of the sea, would arrive, and then finally the sea itself.

And Ed, anticipating this, said, "When we get to Stanford, Dad, how long will you be able to stay with me?"

"Not long. Probably just a few hours."

"A few hours? I was planning on a few days—to show you around, while I register."

"I'd like to, Ed. All I can say is that I would be too worried to enjoy myself."

And the next morning—after they had stayed at a stucco motel with a rose light above the wrought iron, with a neon martini glass above the roof—they would find themselves in a corridor of redwoods, Ed remembering a diagram he had seen as a child—THE OLDEST LIVING THING—presenting the overpowering sequoia in all its stages with adjoining scenes from history, with Sophoclean dancers, appropriately masked, gesturing above the tree in its early growth; they would pass, in the corridor, glimpses of the rock-studded sea like hung pictures, until the sights would merge into a vast seascape showing the mammoth white crescent of the shoreline, which would give way, as the road changed, to a second grey country of madronas and scrub oak, a land dwarfed by geysers and colossi of clouds, and at the end of these floating planes, San Francisco would arrive suddenly, only to be hidden again beneath late afternoon fog and the lock-and-key arabesque of wrought iron.

"Here—take Mom's packet home with you," Ed would say, seeing the Palo Alto hills coming into view.

"No—I might lose them. I'm in a hurry. Give them to her at Christmas."

And arriving at the sandstone college on a late Saturday afternoon, they would take a walk up to the campus lake where, under forest fires of cloud, the trees would spread their autumn light through the water, and, with the corridors darkening with webs of shadow, the whole sunset would seem to fall upon the mirrors of the lake in a golden hail. The wind would beat the windbreak, and, turning back, they would pass under the cornices of a library where medieval emblems would dance, bargain and swoon, their conjuror's globes seeming to spin like gyroscopes.

"You'll be happy here," his father would say.

"Before you go, let me show you where I'll be. I've got my schedule and room numbers."

And through the lamplight, laced with oak leaves, they would move from building to building, from empty room to empty room, until his father would finally turn to the car and light his pipe. For the first time, Ed would look at the smoke and notice it. It would be rising, arching, whitening as if with cold. "Suppose," he would say, "I don't make it—I don't keep up my grades, so they won't let me stay at school."

"You will," his father would say.

"How do you know I will?"

"Because you'll do it for me."

The flames in the sky would be burning down low, to the rim, and there would be the smell of leaves. Clouds and stars would be rolling in from the city, and the moon, gaining some color, but still only a flicker of light, would come brooding out of the vault and descend slowly above the forest and planes, long-winding, of construction wastes. And he would be waving good-bye.

Ed, looking at him now, knew he would never be the same.

"Mom?"

"Ed—good of you to call. Somehow, I thought you would."

"Are you alone? Where's Dad?"

"He's still at the hospital, Ed. I just got back."

"I thought they were going to let him come home."

"No, not yet."

"How is he?"

"Well, Uncle Marl and I were just there, and we both thought he looked better."

"So he made the transfer from Portland O.K.?"

"Yes."

"You know, I was never sure from your letters—how did he ever get in Portland?"

"He was on his way back from St. Louis—driving of all things. Your father—but I can't explain all of that over the phone. I'll write you again."

"How does he feel?"

"Well, he doesn't say. They've got him pretty well doped up right now. The doctors are working hard to keep him quiet."

"Have they had trouble?"

"Not trouble—but these tensions keep coming back. Business tensions. Thinking about how much this is costing is hard on him when he knows he hasn't got a job."

"How much is it costing?"

"Last week it was $1100."

Ed hesitated—nearly his father's half of the tuition.

"The insurance will cover part of it, but what keeps bothering Dad is that once he's out, he'll have no retirement. And he's got to be in the hospital another three weeks—that's what Dr. Kraft told me today. I guess he's at the crucial stage—where the heart is healing. And then when he does get out it'll be another six weeks—at least six weeks—of rest here at the house."

"And that makes it even harder on Dad," Ed said.

"Yes, and I can't see how I'll be able to help him. He said something the other day—yesterday I think it was—about you having Granddad's memoirs and having you send them home. Does that make sense?"

"Yes," Ed said. "We talked about them in the car. I'll send them."

"I don't know, Ed. I sometimes wonder if anything will do him good. Maybe when you get back, you'll find some way."

"I hope so," Ed said, wavering. Then: "Mom, another reason I called was I wanted to know about Thanksgiving."

"Yes, honey."

"Do you want me to come up?"

"Well, that's up to you."

Ed waited another moment, feeling the expense, and listening to the nervous eddies in the long distance background.

". . . it would be wonderful to see you," she said, as if despite herself.

"But it would be an extra expense."

"Yes," she said, "I sort of checked around, and the best way you could do it would be to get a train from Oakland for $26.50."

Ed still couldn't decide. Did her precision mean she thought of the trip as another burden? Or maybe she'd been waiting and hoping he would come, and that was why she had checked on fares.

"No," he finally told her, "that's really too much."

No response.

"Christmas break," he went on, "is only a month or so away, so it really won't be that long until I see you."

"Well," she said, "you could go to Shirley's. Last time she wrote, she said she would be delighted to have you."

"Are you sure?"

"Positive."

But she seemed to be waiting to say something else.

"Mom," Ed said, "you've got to tell me something. When you wrote that letter first telling about the heart attack, what did you mean about the 'good news'?"

"I'm afraid I don't remember."

"You wrote something about me not coming home and that Dad would rather I stay here, then come home at Christmas with the 'good news.' Is Dad depending on me?"

"Depending on you?"

"Yes," Ed said, wondering if he would ever make himself clear. "Does he think that I'm going to come home with some good news about my grades or something that will make him feel better?"

"Well, if you mean the problem of the grade reports—I haven't told him about them. It must be awfully competitive down there."

"Yes, it is. Just yesterday I had to drop a course. But competition isn't the reason I'm doing so badly." He could tell his mother was anxious to know the reason. "I guess it's because I can't keep my mind at it. I'm learning a lot—maybe too much, but it doesn't show. And I'm trying to condense everything into the C.O. statement."

"Do you have to worry about that now?" she asked. Her tone was becoming sharper, as if to signal an end. "You know how Dad feels about you disrupting your education."

"Yes, I know."

She still waited, however.

"Mom, how are you feeling?"

"Well, Ed, I don't seem to get to bed very well these nights," she said. "I don't sleep too well. I guess it's because I miss Dad. The days he feels good, I sleep like a log, but the days he feels bad, I can't help but have that on my mind. The other day they gave him an insulin shot for his diabetes—"

The operator interrupted.

"Diabetes?" Ed asked hurriedly. "I didn't know he had diabetes."

"Yes," she said, also hurriedly. "Diabetes and pneumonia were two of the complications."

"I wish I had known," Ed said.

"Why?" she asked. "You've got enough to think about."

"Well, anyway, what happened?"

"The insulin gave him trouble with his eyes," she said. "And, Ed, it scared me."

Ed fought back a vision of their house—leaded panes and the empty autumn yard perfectly still in the afternoon—only shadows along the fences—and his mother sitting there and asking for help.

"Don't worry," he said, "by Christmas, things will be better. I'm thinking of quitting Stanford after this quarter and going to work—for just a little while."

"Just take it a quarter at a time," she said. "I think if he knows this Christmas you've had a good quarter, that'll be a big boost to him."

"Well, I'll have something to show for it," Ed promised.

"I'm sure you will. And we'd better get off."
"O.K.," he said. "Well, it won't be long."
"No," she said.
"Well, good-bye. Send Dad—my best."
"I'll do that, honey."

Silence. Long distance eddies. The operator came back on and told him his overtime. He hadn't felt free to call collect.

He came out of the phone booth and walked across the quadrangle and then further on, northward, through the thickets of eucalyptus, to an abandoned courtyard left islanded, virtually a century prior, by an earthquake. There was a tree leaning against the stone bench and overspreading the rubble fountain, a tree like the one he had seen in the frontispiece of a Renaissance volume of Plutarch, its bark drying and aging in the shining overcast, like parchment. He had come here for weeks, now, to read his Virgil and Euclid, to prepare his poems and drawings for the student journal—which had eventually accepted them. Then one afternoon: "We regret to say that this fall issue of *Workshop* suffers from its perennial plague of verbosity. Edward Hill's 'prose poems'—if they can be called that—are clearly vitiated by a murky Christian symbolism that only an adolescent could make heads or tails of. 'The Swan Sequence,' the first, is an ecstatic view of what we presume is both a city and yet mythopoeic world. Then in waltzes Dionysus and everything is changed, miraculously, into a medieval cathedral of Thomistic prose and Aristotelian dialectics (we suppose). Then we have the tumble down of the church and what can be guessed to be the modern age of isolation, rising up from the ashes, as embodied in the terse story, 'Persephone,' and its postlude, 'The Prologue.' What we can conclude from all this is that, alas, Mr. Hill is a freshman and in much need of English 1. Perhaps after a bit of bonehead work, he can then emerge from his closet and begin talking to us instead of solely to himself."

His mother had written, "Ed—Dad was glad to get your

letter—I read him a few snatches of it in the hospital. But he isn't sure he understands all of it. The part about making all of your work fit together. He was afraid you were being too idealistic—trying to make one course lead into another. Maybe, Ed, that's why you're having trouble with some of your courses? I have to admit it scares me thinking of the time you also said you were spending on Draft work. Are you protesting the War? And if so, what are the dangers? Please be careful."

He had decided that his failure had come even before the review in the *Stanford Daily;* he had been sitting trying to formulate an accurate translation of an ablative absolute, the Virgilian phrase forming, however tenuously, the cross-beams of Dido's unfinished temple, when—it had slipped from his attention. All his revisions and drawings had become confusion. The news of his father had arrived, and in trying to guess what had happened, he had found he had lost the ability to put sentences and lines together, the sheets becoming a ridiculous melee of attempts, of assays, pencilled and inked a hundred times over, especially after he had tried to visualize his structures.

He had sat in his Latin class—they had now jumped to the Fourth Book—and had been perfectly aware of Mercury passing Atlas, his shoulders supporting the world in an arc of suffering, his beard thick with frost-covered pines and—ATLAS CLEANERS—Ed had been able to see through to his father's journey—to his entering Foley's office, having it out with him, being fired, and then, without telling anyone, renting a car and taking his journey westward, nearly reaching home but being stopped in Portland, where the heart attack had broken him.

Sitting in English class, he had listened to the discussion of "The Tail" chapter in *Moby Dick* and had become obsessed with the notion of *sana mens in sana corpore,* of Goethe's chest being arched like the vault of heaven; for the night before he had dreamed that he and his father had been badly made, with hearts planted deep within them that ticked and clucked like poorly made clocks; and Ed, surrounded in class by magnificent specimens of manhood, had wondered how they, both he and his father, could recover their strength.

"You must get up," he told himself—and he left the courtyard. "Tie all the loose ends together. Get your C.O. statement down on paper—do something active, assert yourself—protest. It might be pleasant to be a monk in a cloister, but it is also irresponsible."

He made his way to the Administration Building, to the special office for Selective Service—the liaison. At the cage, he said, "I want you to know I dropped a course."

The secretary got up from her desk. "Fine. What is your name?"

He told her.

"You know we automatically get a report once the card goes through. Do you have any special reason for telling us?"

Ed hesitated. "I thought I was obligated—"

"We are," she said. "At least that's what the General tells the universities. But—" She was still observing him strangely. "The rules don't state clearly that we have to go out of our way. That is, unless your board specifically asks us, they can still think you're carrying a full load."

Ed's voice was upon him. "But that would be getting away with an ambiguity. The truth is out, so you'd better tell them."

Dumbfounded, she agreed.

He spent the rest of the afternoon leafleting the campus and town.

FIVE

The voice on the intercom had to yell several times before he responded.

"Hill—there's a call for you."

At the end of the hall, he found it was his aunt. "Ed, I've just heard from your mother. I've got great news. Your father's up and moving around. And other news, too. Can you come down to San Francisco? We could have dinner and a good long talk. I don't have to leave until later this evening."

"What day is it?" Ed asked.

"Saturday."

"My God, I missed Thanksgiving. What news, Aunt Shirley?"

She was trying not to keep him in suspense. "Your father's become very—relaxed—now. I thought we could have a little time together and talk. Especially since you didn't come for Thanksgiving."

"I'm sorry about that. I was out all night politicking. And then I think I was tear-gassed."

"Ed!"

"It made me sick. I have such lousy lungs. It runs in the family. Shirley, maybe I should stay here."

"You come down and see me. Get some breakfast in you and come."

"I could—since I wait tables, they have to give me breakfast."

"Ed, are you neglecting yourself?"

He smiled, rubbed his hair. "Yes, totally."

"Then get yourself down here."

"O.K., Shirley—"

"When will you be here?"

"Well," he said slowly, "to get myself to San Francisco, I'll have to con some breakfast off of Earl where I usually work. Provided that happens, I'll be there by three."

"See to it that you are," she said with worry. "Take the first bus up. I'll be watching for you."

He made his way slowly into the shower, his body still acrid with tear gas. Shirley's questions were still with him, and he asked them himself. How long had he been in bed? How long since he'd washed? When was the last time he had attended class? He rubbed the back of his neck—he'd been nightsticked, too, but not seriously. First there had been a dance, then a rally, and then a protest. Or had it been the other way around? He remembered: he had been able to visualize his father perfectly. He had been lying in bed, taking medicine. The moon had glowed frigid and white against the window shade, making flowered figurines on the wall—his father had taken no notice. And then the rally had started, and he had lost the image.

Under the warm water, he looked out the window, over the campus. Stanford was rising up, silver-lined, from random pools, like a crystal garden growing in a goldfish bowl. The sandstone planes were mirrored perfectly, even though their counterparts—on the other side of the mirror—were obscured by a mist which held tentative rainbows. Half asleep, he felt—even so—still alive and urgent. Perhaps it was Shirley's voice. So—soon the water was off, and he was getting dressed and combed. What was it he was trying to remember—after these nights of continuous yelling and finding strength in numbers? "You are hereby directed to report—" It came upon him again, like the voice he kept trying to escape. How many others among the hundreds would have to go through Pre-Induction at Christmas? How many would fail to report, become delinquent, disappear?

Fail to report—sounded so good. To vanish. And yet to have your whereabouts known, to be expected at a certain time, to be missed and sought out if you happened to keel over: that was even more important. Perhaps that was the feeling he had been trying to recover—knowing that his aunt would be watching for him, now. And just the night before, if the nightstick had come down one degree harder, he might have remained anonymous in some hospital for a week.

But that was not what he had been trying to remember. His shaving completed, he shook his head in the mirror. It had flashed by him—like a starling past the window—when he had looked out at the mirrored sandstone campus, which rose like a gateway to the city, his mother's city, northward.

LITRA PRIMER—the packet Mrs. Webb had entrusted to him. He must take it into the city and show his aunt, who would remember, must remember, all of it. It must be the first thing to go in his bag—along with his shaving case; for Shirley would want him to sleep over.

In the alley, he walked to the old chateau dormitory where he washed dishes. In the evening, after work, he would sometimes sit in the courtyard of the building opposite, listening to the fountain and the rush of piped water, in and out of Old Union. Sometimes, after the night and fog would arrive—the net curtains becoming nothing but mist on the panes—he would slip inside, to study. That had been before the war protests had begun. And sitting there, in the Victorian parlor, he could see Earl, the cook, on the other side of the alley, locking the kitchen door in the porchlight and walking out to his shack, behind the chateau, hearing—Ed was sure—pockets of sounds in the branches, motions of shadows, left by squirrels and rabbits, hurrying among the leaves. One light would be waiting for him at the shack. Swing of screendoor—latticework of light, the door swinging to, and the huge window facing the alleyway, across from Old Union courtyard. And Earl, Ed knew, would wait for the sounds of Saturday night to begin: sometimes a random truck, a bus (from where?). And then the fraternity would start in with its records—the music, as he had declared, always having something to say to him. Getting up, he would turn on the television, without the volume, because he would be waiting—still—for the sounds.

"Where have you been?" Earl said in the kitchen. "We needed our breakfast washer."

"I was at a rally," Ed said, raising his voice to meet Earl's one good ear. The colossal cook seemed to brood down on him, like a cheerful white shadow.

"That's a bad business," he answered, frowning over his omelet. "You don't have your parents to direct you, so you're letting yourself get mixed up in all kinds of stuff." His black face was stark, momentarily. "Do you understand what I'm saying? I used to do that when I only used to see Gretta once a month maybe instead of once a week. She used to say to me, 'Now, Earl, you get your head on straight and stop neglecting yourself.' And that's what I'm saying to you now, Edward. You can have an omelet here everyday of your life as long as I'm here, whether you work here or not—because you're one of my boys—but if you're going to get yourself straight, you have to do yourself the service of showing up."

"I've been ordered to report," Ed yelled. "Pre-Induction Physical—Seattle—December."

Earl waited a moment, turned the omelet in the pan that never showed a mark, in the skillet that always held the thin and perfect shell of oil. "Now don't go pulling no heroism. Don't you think I know? I see that bruise. You get yourself up to that Pre-Induction and then you find some way of coming back here. But don't go pulling no heroism. Or if that doesn't work, get your ass up to Canada. So that sometime later you can put yourself back down here. And your omelets will be waiting just like they've always been. But don't you go thinking about prison. And I can tell you have. And I hear what some of the students have been saying—and I know they've been talking like it's something special—gives them status. But it isn't that way, Edward, it'll get you nowhere—" He finished the omelet, placed it on the white glaze of the plate.

"Well, I haven't made up my mind yet," Ed told him.

"And that's just what you ought to do," Earl said, setting the omelet in front of him. "Make up your mind. I've got three boys of my own (I'm going to see them tomorrow night—Edward! One of them's going to be singing solo in an oratorio in a church in San Jose). I saw you out in the alley, a few weeks ago, running your head off trying to catch up with some athlete. Everybody has got talent, Edward, of a special kind. With my three boys it's different—each one. What do you want to be, Edward?"

"An architect," Ed said.

"Then be it—don't go screwing around with this other stuff." He went out to the back hallway to unlock the refrigerator.

When he came back, Ed said, "I wish I could do what your son is doing, Earl, giving his father something to be proud of by singing like that. How old did you say he was?"

"Nineteen, Edward." But his face changed; he sat down. "But you know, Edward, Gretta—she works in a doctor's office down in Berkeley, and you know I can't see her all week. And she called me last week—she said she had a miscarriage. I missed the boat, Edward. That's it. Having children makes you feel younger."

"I don't know what to say—but your three boys—"

"They'll be grown soon," Earl said. "Then what? I'll be home for good, Edward. Gretta and I will live in the same place." His face changed again. "And it'll be just like that tomorrow night," he said cheerfully once more. "Like we were always together. I missed Thanksgiving, Edward, but I've got two days off. Sunday and Monday."

"So there's just today to wait through."

"Oh—and I don't worry about that. I've got me a newspaper and a late show on television. And before you know it, it'll be Sunday afternoon, and Gretta and Henry coming down the walk to take me to the concert." He held Ed's shoulder for a moment. "And you—I want you to start showing up here after this weekend. And getting your breakfast."

"Yes, Earl." He returned his grip. "I will."

Having taken the bus into San Francisco, he stood waiting for the cablecar on Market Street.

And there was a woman high in a window, between the stucco Aloha Theater and the high flight Town House apartments, adjusting her Venetian blinds, showing, each time, the marvelous pots on the windowsill. And below, between the openings and closings, the traffic moved past, the cablecars chiming, all sounding—as the fog clouded the cold November light—not like the sea but the imitated sound of the sea in an inverted shell.

Why did he feel elated? And he went on watching the anonymous woman adjust her blinds—yes, he could see, she was old—nearly eighty—and with every adjustment, the bay window changed, the rococo designs along the eaves changed. And in a café on street level, a capped frycook was adding Crisco to the grill, and the patties were going down in a hiss, with the buns browning on the side, the meat buckling.

On the M car—suspended by a strap, he said to himself, "The voices are gone," and he thought, "The most beautiful word there is is 'timber.' " And suddenly he could smell the burnt sawdust from the incinerators in Westburg, Washington, just as he and his father were driving through with all the windows open—and he knew he had been wrong about Collier; there was no Jonsonian resonance in his voice; there was nothing of the Jonsonian workshop about him. His poems held nothing of the smell of wood. They were all handicrafted American artifacts—souvenirs. It was as if in avoiding the smell of the lamp, Collier had turned to mining in various Indian burial grounds—had come up with some dazzling bits of turquoise, broken pottery, even polished bone. But what were they to Collier or Collier to them? He had sunk the wrong mine shaft and missed his own ancestry.

"And so this is my ancestry," Ed said ironically but still feeling elated. "The neon martini glass above the Twin Peaks tunnel." And in a moment they were in a breathless darkness, re-emerging into random fog and evening sun, softened in the corners of palm branches. "Stonestown," the driver said, and the shuttle emptied. Ed, still holding onto the strap and watching the passengers leave—like Earl they were a part of the innumerable homeward returning Saturday workers—was able to catch again his own translation of Boethius from the first weeks—unspeakably serene —at school—

> Masterbuilder of the star-hung universe
> Who, enthroned in the swift rotation of eternity—

And he could not believe that all had occurred so quickly, that just a few months before he had been driving downtown on a July evening, picking his father up at work and having dinner out at the Norse House Smorgasbord. What had come in between? They had gone up to a lake in the Cascades and then driven through the hallowed redwoods, whose darkness had been more breathtaking than what they had been through only moments before. And now, with the cablecar cleared, he was sitting down next to a reader of "the superb and brilliantly conceived romance," *Crimson Clouds Beyond the Curtains*, and trying to shake free of the blankness of the night before.

He held his mother's packet in front of him. LITRA PRIMER. And inside: "an accidence for the student preparing for high school and college. Ed., Ed. M. Hill." The cablecar swung them heavily to a stop. Up ahead, just prior to Ocean Avenue, the total belt of fog lay brewing, with only the neon turret—distant—of the El Rancho Theater hovering above to mark his stop.

"I must be imagining," Ed thought and was, momentarily, afraid to look again. But it was there—the name of the man who must be his grandfather. The coincidence was almost too startling to mention—and there was the title of his mother's school district—BALBOA—stamped in the corner: Balboa School District #1. And there were the major stories: Don Quixote, Aeneas, Achilles, Odysseus, Faust—all with appropriate post-Victorian engravings. And major selections: Shakespeare, Dante, Milton.

> So high above the circling canopy
> Of night's extended shade, from Eastern point
> Of Libra to the fleecy star that bears
> Andromeda far off Atlantic seas—

Holding the book tight—as if the evidence might be gone by the time he reached Shirley's—he walked to the back of the car and got off under the turret: "Ocean Avenue," the driver said, seeing him.

But the avenue was soon gone; he was making his way, following a recollection of five years prior, through a brief park of camellias, whose flaring pink appeared momentarily through the tumble down of mist. Shirley's house was on the other side—although he couldn't see it yet. First there was his uncle's cathedral, its unlit stained glass all beads of water—and then there was the porchlight of the house next door and the address which he had written down in Seattle.

"Ed," his aunt said, unlocking the gate. "Come in—you don't look at all well—not at all like yourself."

"How would you know?" Ed asked, smiling, as he followed her inside. "You haven't seen me in years."

"And it's a wonder you found this place. I would have driven into town to pick you up. But you know I don't drive." She shook out his coat and hung it up. "I told your mother again and again to have your father bring you here before school started but it never seemed to get through."

He sat down in the living room. She had a fire going. Just as he remembered—the tables were covered with French classics, all in white covers. "Dad was so preoccupied," he said. "I just don't think he could bring himself to stop."

His aunt had already sat down with a letter in her lap. He recognized his mother's handwriting and wondered if she was holding it as some kind of evidence.

"Now what sort of thing have you been involving yourself in?" she asked. "I worried when I heard this morning."

"We stormed a building that's associated with napalm," Ed said. "That's when the tear gas came."

"That makes a lot of sense," she said. "More violence."

"No—no one was in the building at the time."

"But there's no telling you anything—because you have your father's stubbornness. I can see that." She smiled and fell silent, holding the letter in reserve.

"There is the strangest coincidence," Ed said, breaking the pause and wanting to change the subject. "I just found that my grandfather—on Dad's side—was the editor of one of Mom's old school books. I just happened to look at it on the streetcar."

"Wherever did you get that?" she asked, taking it.

"Marlice Webb gave it to me to pass on to Mom. She had been saving all of these various relics."

"Yes, yes, I remember Marlice"—going through—"we were all of us at Balboa Polytechnic. Did you know it was at about that time your mother showed such musical promise?"

"Yes."

"She had one of her first recitals right in back of us—at the cathedral. And she had a great many others as well. We all wanted her to study under Slatoff, who was living in San Francisco at the time. But then she met your father. Fresh from the Midwest and sent by the Company."

Ed smiled. "A destined encounter."

She nodded without humor. "Yes, of course. But what's happened leads me to say now—although I never would have thought of saying it to my nephew before—it was one of the most miscast marriages I've known."

"There have been some battles," Ed said. "But I wouldn't call it miscast."

"But you should be aware how our mother pushed."

"Against it?"

"No, no—against your mother's talent. She was moving in that very underground Berkeley set at the time, and your grandmother was terrified, because there was talk of taking a long tour into Russia—with some possibility of inculcation—and then here Tom comes up the family walk—with some five years of salesmanship behind him and money in the bank and a big promise in the Northwest!"

"So I could thank Grandmother for my existence," Ed said. "If she were around."

"You have some interesting collisions in your history," his aunt said, avoiding his irony and returning the book.

"Yes—and I wanted—"

"And I wanted to mention your mother's letter."

Ed waited. "Yes, I think I know about it already—Dad's up and around. At least, Mom said we could expect it."

"Yes," his aunt said, "but your mother's worried about him.

"Why?" And yet Ed knew his naiveté was transparent. "I was told the worry point was passed."

"Did you know," she asked, "that there is a whole week unaccounted for—as far as your dad going to St. Louis is concerned?"

"It takes a long time to get fired," Ed said. "And then he had to drive back."

"He was fired the same day he arrived." His aunt held up the letter. "He could have been home virtually the same night if he'd wanted to. But, no, he had to take some great cross-country trip by car and drive your mother crazy with worry while he was doing it. Nobody knew where he was—not even his own sister in St. Louis."

Ed felt he knew the reason why. And he felt he should have been at home. To explain to his mother.

"How she handled that worry I don't know. She says here

that she can't account for whole days herself. Some days she would find herself in the middle of the city and not be aware of having taken the car—or the bus."

"Yes, yes," Ed said, "she just wanted to be alone." And he could see his mother clearly, now, taking the bus over the Jutland bridge, while his father drove through the last copse of trees in Jamestown, North Dakota.

"When your uncle was alive," his aunt said, "I knew every day of his life where he was. I could see him perfectly through these windows—in his office, in the sacristy, or wherever. I don't know what I would have done if one day he just happened to vanish from the pulpit."

The phone rang. "Don't move—I'm going to have some dinner for you in just a minute."

The French doors which she opened were now flaming perfectly with the reflected fire. And he thought of his uncle vanishing—which in fact he had. He had raised his baton (in his dual role of pastor and choir director) above the small, amateur chorale—fanned out in an arc to sing Handel's *Theodora*—and the heart attack had taken him. It might have seemed even comic at first. Like Finnegan falling from the ladder. Only, in this particular catastrophe, his Uncle Merlin had danced off a podium.

His aunt returned. "That was my ride. She'll be taking me up to see Merlin's mother. I wish I could stay, but I have to go when the rides are provided. Anyway, you can stay here. I wouldn't want you trying to catch an M Car on the streets after dark. Far too dangerous—" She had become distracted and nervous with the thought of her journey. "Originally I was going to have us go to a small café—really it's in a lady's home—at five. You can even see it from here—so there's no danger. We could have walked together, and of course, when you're with someone it's safer. It's like a tearoom, but this woman runs it in her home. She uses real linen tablecloths. When I had heard you had been tear-gassed. To think of it—and then of course I didn't even ask how you were, because I was thinking about this letter. I thought we should go to the tea room. But then I called. The woman closes at five on Saturday."

"Never mind," Ed said. "It'll be just right here."

"This war, this war," his aunt said, ignoring him. "To think of you in a protest, to think of the constant danger. My God, what is happening? Your mother and I just sitting in our houses. I was going to go up and see her, but she wanted to be left alone. That's all we do—we women—we just sit and wait for something terrible to happen." She wiped away tears. "To think of these terrible, terrible changes. You just stand at the window waiting for the next unbearable newspaper. And why won't your father stay in one place and appreciate what he has? Pretty soon your mother's going to be alone herself and then what?"

Ed, completely astonished, said, "But, Aunt Shirley, he's home now. He's staying in one place."

"But your mother says that he's given up. He doesn't care about living."

"Of course," Ed said quickly, "anyone would feel that way at first." But he was terrified, having suspected it all along.

"Maybe so, maybe so," she said, getting up and leading him out of the room. "But why would a man just give up like that? That's what scares your mother. Your uncle, when he died, was still going strong."

"It sounds like everyone's after him," Ed said, still following her. "When you work for forty years with no vacation you're entitled to a little aimlessness."

Still frightened, he sat in silence while Shirley brought the food; she had opened the curtains to a back view of the foggy cathedral.

"You'll have to finish out the dinner yourself," she said finally. "I have to leave in a matter of minutes."

"Didn't Mom have any good news at all?" he asked. "I thought you said there was some."

"They've been able to meet their bills for the transfer

from Portland," she said. "And now that he's up and about, they can start to recover financially."

"Then you shouldn't," he said, "have him dead already. He'll take care of himself. If not just now, eventually."

She shook her head, balled up her napkin. She was holding herself down—away from what had happened before. "You've got to understand, Ed, that I've never been fair to your father. There's always been a friction between us. Your mother and I were close, and I always thought she would stay where we could be together."

The car was outside.

"Listen, Ed," she said, getting up. "I want to give you something before I leave. If you ever need to come down to the city just to get away, and I'm not here—here's a key."

Once she had taken it from the mantlepiece and had stopped for a moment in the hall, she was gone. He heard the wrought iron lock into place. And then, shut in with the view of the cathedral, he ate and later slept with the fog tightening its circle about the house. The cathedral disappeared—but from the bedroom, he could hear the ivy-entwined belltower drip its grey water onto the stone. He dreamed of the city as a vast thesaurus, a book but also a treasure house to which he held the key. And his father came to him as a man whose heart was a bad clock.

In the morning, he awoke to a lawn and arbor that were a veritable watergarden of sunlight and colors from the rose window. Getting up, he went into the flaring yellow kitchen and read his mother's letter.

PART TWO

THE MASTERBUILDER

At the window, he could see the mountain ash in the yard beyond, and he remembered what his mother had said about the day she had gotten the news. She had sat by the phone, knowing that in a matter of hours it would ring. And the mountain ash, within her view, had seemed to flame hellishly. That had been her word.

"Hellishly"—it had been such a surprise to him, as he had sat there in her apartment, long after his father had died—she telling him of her recollection. And he had said, "I really know nothing about you. Except that you had a hidden talent and helped Dad night and day."

She had answered, "It wasn't planned that you should know anything. Your father and I wanted to appear in agreement while we were raising you."

"And then it all ended when his heart attack came."

"Not at that moment, but during the week he was away."

He now kept, in his own group of Jutland rooms, a drawer full of the family history, and in it was the letter he had confiscated from his aunt years later. "I didn't call the police or the highway patrol," she had written, "because secretly I knew exactly what he was doing."

And in his own walks through the city, to and from the university, where he was now regaining his strength, he could imagine his mother sitting beside the phone and watching the wind whipping off the rain, in lines of drops, the branches still red, hellish, standing out in exact tiers of flame, as if the brick-colored soil were immanent in the leaves themselves. Three o'clock: fringes of heat hang along the register; the sky seems rinsed with old tea. She gets up—takes her coat and umbrella, still trying to define what is happening, about to happen.

Outside, all the way to the Jutland Bridge, Elliott Bay is a flood beneath her, as it presses against the naval yards, which stand as a prologue to the city's center in the distance, a set of buildings placed, seemingly, upon a floating disc, tilting, from time to time, when the wind hits the water. Once across the bridge, she comes to an apartment building with music coming from its windows: two separately moving hoops—piano and guitar—never playing together but never playing in disharmony. She thinks—as she had said later—about selling the house, about life in an apartment: passkeys, mail keys, coin laundry—the sounds of people above and below—never enough light. She passes, now, every building her father ever managed, from the time she was four until the moment she moved away from home: a continual line of transiency from the brownstones in New York to the two-story stuccoes with the rosette lanterns in San Francisco.

At the corner—and now far removed from the water—she stops and waits at a bus station. Across the street: a basement beauty shop—Queen Lion's. Three lithographs. Three hairstyles, all from the back. A bus comes—and through the window, which ripples with water shaken from eaves and trolley wires, she sees gilt lettering within a square of momentary sun, and neat shadow prints on the glass. And then all the city's violence seems to press itself upon her.

Bus starts, slows again. Snapping of blinker. Bus driver's arm out the window, just to make sure. Rain dotting his sleeve. Pressure brakes clamping, bus rolling into the next lane, the neon plaque of the drugstore razorsharp in the overcast, the driver still signalling, swinging over and releasing the doors, waiting for the kerchiefed woman.

"Sound's end?"

"What?" the driver asks.

"Sound's end?"

"What?"

"Is that where you're going to?"

"No"—with the door slamming. He flips the wheel in furious roulette, almost demolishes the tailgate of a news truck, turns on the wipers, which squeal across the random drops. He plays chicken with the street signals, waits dead center in a backed up intersection with the traffic arriving from all four sides, signals and blinkers winking inanely.

Then the coast, free, down the hill, rain furious now. The breakers hitting the docks. One car plows into another, rising high over the back windshield. She pulls the cord to transfer, to return a different way.

Rain, umbrella open. Some sun. Across the street: the empty stadium. The wind hits the leaves like hell, and the lean-to bus station provides no resistance. The leaves, rising in a cluster, atomize like flocks of aimless birds. The fountain at the center of the university sends out a continual bloom of rapids, which ripple, oblique angles, when the gales smash the stone bowl.

The man sitting next to her holds a paper: D^+ in red. Not looking at anything, not even the flying ribbons of leaves, that snap into painfully exquisite whips. Veins of grey in his sideburns—and the clouds roll off the mountains, a slow-moving avalanche. Across the street—the tires over pavement; children turn a bottle end-over-end from a bridge. "Bio 572" up in the upper left hand corner, and still the wind and sun through the branches, creating a silver violence.

She gets on a second bus, wondering what happened to her earlier distantness. The driver swings her up and over three hills, gets rid of her along with the others. She watches them plod ahead of her, secretive under their umbrellas.

At home, it is still there, the bus ride and its pressure of light. Sitting again by the phone, she begins to type, and as the sound repeats itself, in brittle precision, she thinks of a man slugging a punching bag, flapping it and flapping it and flapping it, the shadows swinging like hanging lamps, and the sweat brimming, and the heat widening down the back, and the teeth, sharper, harder now against the lips, and the thud, inane, egging him on to slug it, slap it some more, and she thinks of Tom outside, building something, sawing, his leg rigid against the wood as he uses the porch for a brace, heaving his slackened muscles into the hard push, sweating more, damning the sun, trying to finish before they would have to leave; and then the sawing is finished, and then she knows what is next—that he will have to drive the nails, and so he drives the nails, getting furious with her interventions, slamming the wood until it breaks, and he has to saw again, even though the evening has come and gone, and the party has already started—the hosts wondering where they are—and he is wheezing from the sawdust and the sweat is chilling his shoulders, and he pounds the wood as if he were pounding the dank earth. And she watches him through the screendoor, hating him, his mindless drive, and feeling frozen by the sight of so much energy. Made inarticulate. And when he finally lies down shirtless on the couch and she sees the cruel thongs of sunburn, she wants, unspeakably, to go at his skin with her nails.

She gets up, still with the phone at hand. Making dinner, she thinks of Tom's father—"Why Edward," she had said, "you know I don't read Latin."—and of the ways she had felt a greater ease with him than with Tom himself.

"My dear, my dear. Only from translation, as I have prepared myself."

"How long has it been since I've read these things? Far too long."

"And if only you would learn Virgil! What pleasure it would bring you. Virgilian hexameter! It is like hearing nature grow and return to the soil."

And she remembers the last years, after he had begun to fail, the times she walked him to the toilet, his pants dripping with urine, of the way he looked so humiliated at first, and of how he became tender, later, when he realized she had decided not to notice. And when Tom returned from his next sales trip, she had watched the distantness on the two sides of the triangle begin to widen, as she and Edward drew closer. Tom would have nothing to do with his father's slow failure. And when he had finally borne his father's body back to St. Louis, she gradually came to think of it as statuesque—the train becoming a formal cortege of stops, in Montana, North Dakota, Wisconsin, and later—after the transfer—Illinois, and finally Missouri, a cortege of backwater towns with black-mouthed streams, of Tom's inces-

sant worrying, his mind never settling until he had seen his father into the grave and not even after that.

The phone rings. It is night.

"Mrs. Hill? This is Judith Michaels. I work at Multnomah General Hospital. In Portland. Your husband has just had a heart attack, and is here now and we feel you should come as quickly as possible."

Outside, the first breaths of fall from the wall of acorn, behind the garage. Smell of rainwater, as if from stagnant barrels. Rope of fog dissolves slowly below the moon. She remembers going through town—The Empress Theater and The Showbox—and then nothing else, until reaching the moonlit smokestacks twinkling above the Columbia.

She walks into the hospital room. He is mounted on an apparatus which twists tubes about his face. She can say nothing. He takes her hand, but his grip offers nothing—no passionate recollection of who she was or is. He only says, "I knew you would come. I was waiting for you here. It seems to me I have seen thousands of men in a thousand different parts of the country during these last weeks. The kind of men who live in the Midwest, who stand in front of their buildings before going back to business. In their shirts and ties. Waiting for the wind to start up in the trees, and there's dust in the air—and they know the rain's going to be hitting the willows—and they don't even care if they scare away the trade if they stand in their entrance ways like that" —he starts to laugh—"because it's theirs, they've earned it! They've earned it!"

SIX

With his son waving to him from behind the glass, Tom started the car and headed out of the university. It must be his mainstay—knowing he was there.

He drove straight on through, with only two stops, getting to Seattle and Wymansales by noon. He left the car on the Second Avenue lot and took the back entrance—the scrolling of the gilt letters—OFFICE—clear, startling, now, after the rains of the night before.

At the switchboard, Mrs. Carole had left two messages—there was a special delivery letter (St. Louis) ready for him when she reopened the cage at one; also a note from Jamison saying he was out on a sales call but would be back shortly. "Therefore," he said to himself, "the office will be empty. I'll have to go it alone. I've never liked that." And he thought of calling Karin, but he knew she was at work, and he wanted to keep her there: like Ed, moving in a sphere, entirely free, unaware of him.

On the eighth floor: he turned the key in the lock, the wire grate rattling as he pushed back the glass. Next door, the soap salesman—who had had his face put on the black-and-white cover of *Life* magazine—said, "Phone's been ringing all day. I hope you're doing something to take care of it." And there it was—his own colorless replica, hanging on the wall in back of him.

"You better believe it," Tom said. "I'm packing my bags."

"Right—spring sample time. Jamison's been making ten runs a day on the freight elevator. Whole back alley's stacked high with boxes."

"No doubt," Tom said—and shut the door on him while

he was still talking. Dropping his coat and briefcase, he pulled the entire Samuel Webb file, a good two inches thick, dating all the way back to 1939, when all had been arranged. The insignia on the contract was the same West Green tree Webb had scrolled out in emerald neon above his store, sparing no expense.

And there must be a letter to add: "Tom—as per your inquiry about S. Webb, we do verify that the phase-out does include him. You should please be advised that Webb will need to carry a new line by April 1 of next year.

"Will be calling you soon to tie up loose ends.

"As ever,

"E. Foley."

Wondering over his objectivity, Tom decided, yes, it sounded like Foley was getting ready to ax him, too. It had sounded that way when Jamison had read him the letter long distance, and here was the tangible proof. "Item: I have noted it." Therefore: he must be out of here and on the plane within a matter of hours.

Taking up his folder, hat and coat, he was scooting his briefcase out the door, when he was blocked by Jamison, officeward returning and bearing a copy of Virgil.

"You can't be leaving," Jamison said.

"I just wanted the Webb file—then off to St. Louis."

"Well, you'll have to stop for a minute—Mrs. Carole gave me this special delivery letter to pass on."

"Thanks"—pocketing it.

"Aren't you going to read it?"

"Yes, when I get in the car."

Jamison seemed checked. "You look like you haven't slept in a week."

"True—I drove right on through from Palo Alto."

"And the mud—what happened?"

Tom looked down—he hadn't realized it—but, he was caked to the ankles. "I seem to remember stopping somewhere. Why is it I can't remember?"

Jamison stared at him. "Read your letter," he said.

Tom looked at his pants, at the gilt-bound volume which he knew the older man used for toilet stall reading. ("Hexametric defecation—excellent for the bowels.") He looked at *Life* Magazine, who was more than enjoying this bottleneck at the door. "All right," he shouted, letting everything drop to the floor. "We shall proceed." Opening the letter: " 'As per your second inquiry concerning S. Webb, the decision remains same. As part of procedure which was accordingly initiated, all your accounts have been properly reviewed, and we find some monitoring will be necessary in the future. This will be in keeping with new territorial adjustments. As ever, E. Foley.' He says, 'As ever,' Jamison, but really he means, 'ass ever.' And there's something in this letter that's fucked up, Jamison, and I'm going to find out what it is."

Jamison and *Life* both looked disgusted.

"One of these days, Jamison"—tapping the book with the letter—"you're going to find out there's more to life than rhythmic shitting. And you"—looking at the Oxydol eavesdropper—"you're going to find there's more to life than having some trick store put you on some magazine cover."

"Tom, Tom, you're flying off the handle," Jamison said. "You've got to think through your plan."

Oxydol had shut the door. Slam.

"Monitoring? What is this? Monitoring. Finding the hidden camera? Sending out Foley's son to watch? I don't believe this." He still felt bottlenecked at the door. Ready to explode.

"Look," Jamison said, "you can write a letter. Figure out what you're going to defend. What you're going to do." He touched him. "Look, if you get fired, I get chopped, too."

"What do you care?" Tom said ruthlessly. "You've made your mark as a schoolteacher, anyway. Seems like I always get involved with schoolteachers. My father was one, my wife's nearly one, her sister's always one—the only one left is my brother. So what do you care, Jamison? You're here just to draw Social Security, anyway."

Jamison released his hand. "You bastard. How could you

say that? With me nearly working free just to be around you."

"I'm sorry, Jamison," Tom said. "I take everything back. But I've driven over 2000 miles just thinking this through. I've got to fight these changes."

"We'd manage under Consolidated."

"Manage with what—that's the question—with a bathroom stall scrolled 'Gentlemen' while some St. Louis kingfish sits in here at the front desk?"

"All I can say is," Jamison answered, "is that for all intents and purposes you're sacrificing me to Webb."

"Now I know how I got this mud," Tom said suddenly. "One of my two stops was on a back road on the way to Lake Goheen. I stopped the car and looked at a pond."

Jamison didn't answer.

"I know what you're thinking. You're thinking I've gone distracted—got the bends from driving too far. I heard what you said, I appreciate what you said, but I won't have you blocking me anymore. Step aside, Jamison."

At the elevator, he said to himself, "Within a matter of months, they'll be blackballing me at the men's club. How do I know that?" And he thought how strange it was that he'd never noticed the eagle on the mail chute before; he hadn't even been aware that there was a mail chute—except that he had mindlessly brought letters to a place between the elevators and had watched them drop.

The elevator was slow in coming; he took the stairs. At the mezzanine, just where the wood changed to alabaster, he remembered—it was at five a.m. this morning—that he had walked toward the pond, staring at the circle of lilies which rested, floating, at the center. They seemed to rise toward the clouds of breaking gold, telepathically shouting orders. And all about him were ferns, dilated to prehistoric size.

When Tom got into the lobby of West Green Shoes, St. Louis, Missouri, the receptionist did not seem at all surprised that he wanted to see a vice-president without an appointment. She merely smiled, took up the phone, pointing to a row of plush chairs—reserved, probably, for brass. Tom, following instructions, felt he must clamp himself down; if he didn't, he might buckle from sheer fatigue.

"Mr. Hill?" the Oriental girl held the phone against her.

"Yes?"

"Please go right up." She looked shy and embarrassed, as if she knew why he was there.

"It's been a long trip out," Tom said.

"Yes—" and looked down. "And after the two of you are done, I shall give you coffee."

"Thank you."

On the fourth floor, Hilda, Foley's secretary, grabbed his wrist. "Wait a minute. You're not going in there without saying hello first. What's the matter? You gone snotty on us?"

"How are you, Hilda?" He looked at her but didn't see her as a complete image. "I'm getting distracted," he told himself. Because all he could see was the Hilda he had known when he'd first come to West Green—the one who was crazy about arboretums, solariums, and the Shaw Gardens, where they had made her a virtual patron saint—like a figurine statue—within their hallways of roses.

"Not how am I—but how are you? You look like you need sixteen years of sleep. What's the matter? Didn't your sister let you stay with her?"

"She doesn't even know I'm in St. Louis. Hilda, I'm going to do a very rude thing—I'm going to cut you off and go right into Elden's office."

"Of course."

With his wrist suddenly free, Tom turned down the hall, coming into an office which surprised him with the face of a portly gentleman—a man who outaged him, seemingly, by a decade, even though they had grown up together.

"My God, Tom"—shaking hands in a double clasp—"it's good to see you. I was just thinking when I heard you were coming that it's been seven years."

"I know, I know," Tom said, almost so overcome by a

sense of the past that he forgot why he had come—therefore he noticed his own appearance: jaunty, travel-stale.

Silence.

Foley pointed to his best guest chair, then sat down himself. "You'll have to forgive me, Tom. About those letters. I'm afraid the board's inclined to make mountains out of molehills. Anyway, that's the reason for their curtness."

Tom was still engulfed by a study of Foley's features. They were swollen; their character had given way, snapped. Therefore, his eyes, as if panicked by this facial Armageddon, presented a bright flat shield to the outer world. "Curtness or not," Tom answered, "did you mean what you said?"

Foley held up his brightly-cuffed hands. He said, as if in a moment of weakness, "Tom, I know you. I know when you're going to go flying off the handle. Let me say here and now—I don't want an argument. I still feel that potentially you're one of our most valuable salesmen. So if any hotheadedness comes out of this, it's going to have to be from you."

Tom felt he saw the trick and said, "I still want to know, Elden. Is Webb being cut out? Can he count on West Green for next year? Or does April 1st still hold?"

"You know that West Green is being phased out anyway," Foley answered. "You know that everything will be coming under one label—Pauleze, East Wing, and Alice Brand are out, too."

"Of course I know that. But it still comes to the same difference. Can Webb still carry shoes under Consolidated? Does he still have the loan?"

"Remember now, Tom, I was the one who said everyone is making mountains out of molehills. But, no, Webb will not be able to carry us after April 1."

"Why not?"

"Why should he—his sales are down, the general appearance of his store is trashy—"

"How do you know?"

"We sent a man out."

Tom was stunned; he felt as if all four stories had been cut out from under him. "Without telling me?" he asked.

"Yes. During the board meetings when your defenses of Webb started coming up—those letters—they started asking the question why we should favor anyone on the basis of how long he's been with us. 'Sacrifice' was a word which came up frequently."

Tom was out of his chair, outraged. "But those fuckers have no idea of how good or bad someone is—their memory doesn't go beyond the past twenty-four hours. It's all one gold plaque per day. Twenty or thirty years is like talking about the Stone Age to them."

Foley stiffened, offended on the board's account.

"And I include you, too," Tom added.

"How can you say that?" Foley said, surprised and apparently injured.

"Because I know what you had to offer. When your father used to drive us to work, I'd look at you two from the back seat in that Packard. My God—you never knew what I would have given to have a father like that, who could pass on a potential like that. And now you're writing letters that sound like something out of a dime-slot fortune teller. You're forgetting your original accounts along with your salesmen."

"That may all be well and true," Foley said, panicked and furious—with his visual shield breaking like plate glass—"but if it is, why did you come here?"

"To make a gesture," Tom said, ready for him.

"Well, you've made it," he answered, sarcastically.

"Not quite, I'll say it clearly. Webb has carried your shoes for thirty years—therefore, he deserves another year's grace, even if he is a drunk, even if he is a weak sister."

"And I'll tell you, the company doesn't make special dispensations like that anymore, anymore than it could make the kind of single-store loans it used to."

"Hold on. I'm not finished—and next time you send somebody out snooping on my territory, I want to be told."

"That may be hard," Foley said, the shield returning. He was past his crisis. "Because the territories are being redone."

"What does that mean?" Tom asked.

"It means that Washington—eastern and central—goes to the California branch, along with Oregon, Montana and Idaho."

"And so," Tom said, "I'm being shorn."

"Not exactly, there's still—"

"The shit job," Tom went on, "of Seattle-Tacoma and vicinity—working out of a tiny sub-cubicle on the second floor of Wymansales, with the top brass upstairs."

"However," Foley said, "none of this will take place until after April 1."

"That's supposed to be some consolation?" Tom asked.

"Yes, because there will only be minor monitoring until then."

"What do you mean—'minor'?"

"We will," Foley said, composed, "have to send someone out to check your paperwork."

"You can't be serious."

Foley shrugged. "Like I said, Tom, some of this didn't have to happen—but you took it into your head to defend Webb. Once you've stirred up the snakes, there's no getting them down."

"I can see it now," Tom said, "with one of your high-flight monitors around—I'll be told to go heavy on the fly-by-nighters and go light on the people I've been developing for thirty years. The answer to this is 'no dice.' "

Foley looked relieved and seemed to settle back with the sense of a constructive day.

"But it's obvious," Tom added, "that you're doing all this to whitewash firing me."

"Not true," Foley said, recoiling.

"The whole thing is a test in humiliation—pull enough territory and power away and see if I'll quit. Simple as that."

Foley became restless. "I don't like that word, humiliation," he said.

"Neither do I, and on second thought," Tom said, "I'm going to renege on the quitting and accept your offer—Seattle, Tacoma and vicinity. That's what it was, wasn't it?"

"Yes."

"Well, I think I'll take it—so if you want out, you're going to have to fire me."

"What?"

"Fire me."

"Are you asking me to?"

"Yes"—after a quarter of a pause.

"You're fired."

"Thanks," Tom said, standing up and scarcely controlling his fatigue. "It's a pleasure doing business with you."

He turned into the street, knowing exactly where he must go. The ache in his pulses rocked unsteadily, but, somehow, everything seemed to come to him with clean edges, clear to his sight and touch, like those times when, under the pressure of a headache, he could see sharp loops in his pipe smoke. In the window of an Asian novelties company, he saw a woodblock print of a flower: round and even like a white porcelain cup, with liquid pink at the center. Against it—a red magic vase with a single Arabic character painted on the front in yellow. Up higher, beyond the window, the city seemed to bristle with scrolls of stones, with plaques which said "Est. 1876," Mercuries announcing it on either side. There seemed to be so much going on in the higher parts of the city: "5:47/5:47," "Est. 1888," with a flutter of wings, "Firestone-Blimp/Blimp," "Seven-Up"—in the sky, and in a sign: "Libertia—Muse (um)—Est. 1884."

He went into the Benjamin Franklin Tobacco Shop—his goal until now—and bought some Kools, crisp in the pack. Cigarette, burning light, paper, progress. Still. (Kools, Chesterfields, Old Golds. Old Golds with the majorette legs beneath them.) He went into the humidification room. Door shut. Cellophane covers again.

Outside, he walked straight to the Shaeffer Building, to the second floor, where he knew there was a Men's. On the wall: "Life is a shit sandwich and it's always lunchtime." After a cigarette: why not the Vessels Three? Room, single, fifteen dollars a night. He examined the bottom of his Kools: "Mis"—eagle in the middle—"souri 22, 28. tax paid." Endless puns possible. The ear of the urinal: "Headler Standard Brothers." Breathless at the water fountain, he thought, "Haysley Taylor. A signed city: you could turn it over platelike and find the letters, MSW."

Finding himself on a bus, he watched a drugstore sign fill a neon coke glass. Next door, the Orpheum Theater was just opening up, its dead marquee suddenly spreading out in a rapid green fire. Inside, he knew there was a portrait of an aristocratic flapper, opening her jewel box. And the ceilings, lit by floating chandeliers whose globes were arranged in tight circles, would be one deep sea of Greek, Roman, and Oriental gods, whose arms, legs, chests, whips, tritons, and gavels would emerge erratically from the cornice work—all raging toward the same goal—an emerald-eyed Zeus, who blessed everyone, audience and gods alike.

"I remember going there," Tom said, "every Saturday for two years."

And mentally he sat in one of the theater seats and watched a home movie which his memory had been preparing for him. He was standing in the living room taking pictures of the furniture and noticing for the first time how little light came through the windows. He pulled the Venetian blinds, first open, then up. Still no good. It was the leaded panes. Karin and Ed came in. He took their picture, then developed it. Through the depth of solution, he could see something materializing which he had not seen before, when he had been in the room: the blue of the window. It must have been the sudden cold outside, the freezing of the rain, and the brief clearing, at sunset. But there it was—blue like the halo of a low-burning match.

The bus shook. Against some wires that swung towards

him. Forest Park! That must be it—he must have just missed seeing it, for the green was just disappearing between the corners of the signs. All along the perimeter—the northern perimeter—he and Foley had delivered newspapers together, walking the great lawns to the mansions, to the Tillotson monument, the replica of the Jefferson Memorial, whose reflection floated out on the surface of the adjacent pool.

But there would be plenty of time for that, for revisiting. And he could see himself now, driving across the stretch of night streets, rain-glazed and warm, not only of this city but of others; for he had, for some reason—the blue of the window, perhaps—decided to rent a car and fare all the way back to Seattle, taking in the sights of Dakota, of Montana, into the windshield glass, rushing headily down over the mountain passes, into new towns where the daedal streams embroidered the frontiers in waving lines of green; and he could see himself as he left each town, becoming free of its freight, its reminders.

But there was plenty of time for that. For now, there was this whole initialled city to deal with.

"What time is it?" he asked the businessman next to him.

"Six o'clock."

Good. He got off directly, and, under fresh eaves of stone, walked to the Vessels Three. No luggage—nothing. As far as the doorman was concerned, he had been dropped from the Firestone Blimp. Not even a car to park in the ample underground garage.

Up in his room, he lay down, listening to the pigeons outside the window. He could see—get at—the bristling ancient world of the city better now.

SEVEN

Tom felt, as he lay there, that he had let somebody down. Somebody. He kept his body tight and tried to stay out of dreams. It was the inertia. He was frozen into one position.

And so he was away having a beer at the Fall Creek House, and even though he knew he was in the East, he was assured by everyone that he was in the West, and KINGFISHER TUNA was being branded on Elliott Bay, and he was being swung in a car around Green Lake; he saw Ed throw a newspaper into an alcove of shadow. A wing of cloud fell across a row of estates in the Seattle Highlands, then it receded, like the attack and retreat of a storm.

KINGFISHER. The signs would flash on the water all through the early morning. He was sure, because he had helped Ed deliver papers to the lake-view houses. Not far from the water was the city's center itself, all silver and polished and unspoiled at sunrise, like crafted silver under glass. It reminded him of St. Louis—days when he had been out on the road months at a time. He could remember, again, returning to the Company at 4 a.m. and seeing Forest Park at dawn, its trees as brilliant as gift-shop miniatures, worked in bronze.

And now, as he took his next pill, which would send him skyrocketing upward, first, then suddenly downward; now as he watched Karin take his temperature (he was back at home, he assured himself; he must hold on), waited for her to turn the thermometer to the right angle of light, to pause, disbelieving, and then turn, mock-calm, with "101," he wondered what had taken the starch out of him.

Maybe the thing in St. Louis—but it still seemed inseparable from the illness.

"What?"

"Fire me."

"Are you asking me to?"

Instantaneously: "Yes."

"You're fired."

But now—his mind tried to back up—he couldn't tell in what spirit or tone he had spoken it. There was a chance that during his whole flight to St. Louis, during his rush from the airport, during his talk with Hilda and the receptionist, during his ride on the elevator, even during his approach to Foley's closed door, he had been making himself prone, preparing himself for sacrifice. If it was true, he had to face it. But if he faced it, he would have to say that he had willed losing his job, that he had flung himself at Foley's feet, just so he could make a martyr or hero of himself.

"You feel sorry for yourself?" he asked.

"Yes I feel sorry for myself."

"My heart bleeds for you. You're just going to lie there and rot, like a good zeroed martyr, with your hands crossed on your chest. That right? While you're lying there, I'd like you to have a little listen in: 'Initiative is a word a mile long. It is the energy or aptitude that tends to develop or open out fields. The self-reliant individual with initiative will soon find his way to the front.' That was in the thirties. In the forties you wrote, 'Sincerity is the hallmark of honor and the sure way to a permanent position.' Coupled with the all-time favorite, 'If a salesman knows his line and its relative values—knows his organization—knows his fellow men—knows himself and intelligently applies his knowledge, there is no power on earth that can keep him from succeeding.' In the fifties, we all danced to the music of, 'Greatest strength shall prevail where greatest strain exists. Conditions are never just right. While a lot of us are waiting until everything is perfect, others are stumbling along the road to achievement, travelling an incredible distance in their blundering way.' And in your blundering way, you started to write in the sixties: 'Sometimes I think the wisest—' "

Then Tom got a migraine. It was a magnificent migraine, with no holds barred. It began with a cramp in his forehead, then spread out into a thudding vein which zigzagged just below his eye. He was not blinded exactly; it was just that he saw things in prickly diffusion—everything was effervescent with his suffering. He would look at the desk and instantly veins of mahogany and auburn would stand out on the wood's surface, burning his eyes, then fanning out into vagueness again. He had the sense that all objects were being denuded for him, that he could actually read the centers of their energy, that he owned a bond with the minutest particle in the room.

And beneath curtains of clouds, he was packing his station wagon and driving away: through the narrow alleys of First and Second Avenue (SHOWBOX THEATER)—Seattle—leaving Wymansales behind: the same in 1930's as in the 1960's, the mottled gold of the waterfront, the Sound, reflecting off its windows, the pawn shops and auction barns below, as he set out, heading for the gala opening of WEBB'S/WE'VE GOT IT/WEBB'S, overseen by Jarrett the Magician, who stood on the roof with a microphone and said, "Are you ready for this huge/monumental/meditative/colossal spectacle of shoes/and/good/buys?" "Yes!" from the crowd. "Well, here we go." And with a violent swing of his arms, he signalled all to begin.

And Tom saw himself in the backyard of his home, motioning in a team of mules that was hauling a load of bricks. He was constructing a fireplace, then a church. Sunlight came in through the windows and transformed the finished work into a sacred vault. The entire room turned orange, mixing firelight and sunset—he saw the windows, in stained glass. St. Paul's robe was as deeply purple—"as a grape sucker," Tom said aloud.

His temperature skyrocketed two degrees. His legs stirred beneath the blankets, in an ecstasy of objectified pain. He felt a sudden desire, and shocked Karin by grabbing her wrist when she was still turning the thermometer.

"I know," he said, "if anything would worry you, this would be it."

"It's not that I don't want to," she said, almost laughing, "but let's wait until it's not a surprise."

"I know what you mean. It surprised me, too."

He cleared his bed of his father's memoirs, wondered if he would ever get back to them. The pain kept him from deciding. He lay back, and, watching the window, forced time to accelerate. Within what seemed to be a mere matter of minutes, he succeeded in getting the evening to come. By the time Karin had come back from a telephone call, it was nearly night.

"I'm sorry I took so long," she said. "But it was Jamison Hanshaw, and he had a long message he wanted me to give you."

"Good news or bad news?"

"Good."

Tom didn't answer.

"He says that when you're up and ready, he wants the two of you to go into business together—isn't that a great idea?"

He still didn't answer but watched her closely, angry—he knew she was trying to feed him another panacea. He was sure she thought that all he needed to do was to get back into work and circulation again—then the body's circulation would return to the normal order of things.

"When does Starin say I can stop all this bedrest?"

"Soon"— she nodded. "If you start out easy."

"I wouldn't go in business with Jamison if you paid me," he said, speaking, he knew, out of pain and perversity, but also knowing this would be the way he'd feel once he was better—if he got better.

"Why don't you want to go into business with him?"

"Dear, Jamison is probably the greatest man on earth. But he's also the most possessive. Three days in partnership with him and I'd go nuts."

"Well, you ought to listen, just listen, to what he wants to do. In about a month, he says you should walk over to his house, or ride over, and then the two of you could talk. The Club's going to have a brunch downtown, and after you're done talking, the two of you could go there."

"Already planning, scheduling everything out. If he had had his way, he wouldn't have let me go to St. Louis."

"And he would have been right," she couldn't help saying.

"Thanks for standing behind me."

She was tightening into herself—he could tell instantly. The pressure of his headache had made him hypersensitive to what she was feeling, even though it had robbed him, simultaneously, of all tact. He could almost see the tension and outrage channeling through her neck.

"It's so good to know," he said, giving her a last little wind, "that when you've given up everything, your wife still stands behind you."

"Given up everything," she said, "that's undoubtedly what you've done. You've lain there like a corpse for weeks and had nothing to offer me when you're conscious but belly-aching. So you've had a devastating experience; so have I. I nearly killed myself to get to Portland, thinking you were dead, and when I got there I found you didn't care to see me. So what? So what? That's what I say. I stoop and fuss over you and it only makes you worse. When your father was alive he appreciated everything I did. Everything. When you were away, I had the constant privilege of walking him to the bathroom, with him leaking all the way. Your father. But he could even do that with dignity. You haven't got his grace, his dignity. All you can do is sit there and indulge in the fact that you're rotting. O.K., then, rot."

All the time she had spoken, he hadn't been listening—he had known what she would say—only watching. The veins in her hands had been magnificent, and he had noticed—for the first time—the chill vitality of her hair: not a frozen grey, or a void white, but a hermetic silver, containing a deep fire, like her eyes—ferric blue. Still in his ecstasy of pain, he had looked out at her with a stagemanager's detachment, overpowered by the notion, still, that he had heightened all the effects he had wanted.

Her anger was spent. Tom waited for the guilt.

"I can understand what you mean," she said, finally, "about Jamison. But couldn't you just go see him and use your freedom when Starin gives it to you? I know you don't want to stay in bed longer than you have to."

Tom still looked out at her, wondered if this overheightened awareness of her transparency—and not just hers—would follow him to the grave. "Yes, I guess it would be good to see Jamison."

"Then I can call him back?"

"Please do."

And while she was gone from the room, he lay back and felt the headache drain out of him. He couldn't get over that fence, that question. The puzzlement was giving him too much irony. He tried to focus it again.

"What?"

"Fire me."

"Are you asking me to?"

"Yes."

"You're fired."

"Thanks—it's a pleasure doing business with you."

What had been the spirit of his trip? Still, it seemed to be a spirit of negation, a martyrdom preached by his religion but also condemned by it for its submission.

Finally he went to sleep, moving through heady dreams which all took place in the evening. Next morning, when he awoke, his headache was completely gone. Still, the objects in the room had the same stinging force, bearing a heat which seemed to melt shells—the outer flesh—exposing a vertebra or two in the right light.

EIGHT

"Now that you're well," she said, "I've been thinking about some things."

He was finishing off some coffee and getting ready to run out and catch the Jutland bus, which would take him to Jamison's.

"O.K."

"Do you want to keep this house?"—as if she had been building up to it.

Tom looked around. "I guess we might need some money to keep it?"

"Yes." After much strain.

"Take it easy."

"You sure this doesn't bother you?"

"Positive," he said, thinking of her transparency again. "What you want to tell me is—if we're going to save the house, I need to work. Along with you."

"Probably more than you could handle," she said, angry, annoyed at being found out.

"Well, the truth is, I'm not much in a working mood. I feel great, but because I feel great I don't want to work."

She didn't answer.

Tom checked the time—his first thoughts of a schedule in several months. He made ready to leave, still aware of her strain. She was turning against him, because she thought he was turning against himself. Yet, in quieter times, he couldn't tell which it was: Karin, or that self, belonging to him, which she contained.

"After Jamison and I are through with this brunch, I think I'm going to have a look downtown."

She resisted. "At Wymansales?"

"Maybe"—knowing she thought he'd be attacked by nostalgia—"but most likely just some of the places on First."

And, once he was outside and on the Jutland bus, he understood what he had been suggesting, to himself as well as to her. He was going to pound the pavement. The all-conquering dumped landowner out to save his wife and property. At the club meeting today, they'd probably pity him, give him tips on where to find openings. "It's terrible all over Seattle, Tom." "Don't know when I've heard people talk of a worse recession." "So don't feel discouraged, Tom, if you find you're going to have to wait awhile." "Start it out slow—that'd be best—like part-time watchman."

He remembered a night, a decade ago; he had had dinner downtown and then had gone back to Wymansales to work the rest of the samples. He rang, as usual, for the night watchman to let him in, but—no answer. He heard the bell ring irritably within the office, but was unable to tell if anyone was there; Mrs. Carole had shut the panels. No one seemed to be there, not on all eight floors; and, backing out onto the sidewalk, Tom checked for lit windows. None—and it was only 9:45. Going around to a back entrance, he tried a well-used trick: buzzing up the freight elevator from the basement, getting on and going to the first floor, sneaking through a side entrance, and ending up in the front office. There he could check for messages, then take the passenger elevator up to the sample room. But when the freight elevator finally arrived—it had been moving crazily from floor to floor—and opened, he found the night watchman on it, dead. The corpse had probably been riding fifteen or twenty minutes, before he stopped it.

The bus entered the south district—Tom shifting in his seat and deciding that today was promising to be productive, from start to finish, almost against his will. Jamison, no doubt, was in a renewed conspiracy with Karin to get him back into the swing—a signed partnership over Jamison's carefully made breakfast, script by Karin. She hadn't given up at all. Perfectly clear—that when he had asked her to talk to Jamison a second time, she hadn't turned down the offer at all. Instead, given encouragement. "He isn't himself right now. But in a month or so—" Now, this morning, he had had her running scared. He still wasn't himself. Medications and repairs not quite successful; they couldn't get the heat back into his blood, not enough heat, anyway, to get him to stumble back onto the road to achievement. His own phrase—straight, for thirty years.

Shit, too bad, because he really liked Jamison. Was Jamison a good man? Yes, he was a good man. Was he a really good man? Yes, he was a really good man. Was he something not far from a saint? Yes, that could be said, truly. Was Jamison a man who would do absolutely anything for him? Yes, there was no question of it.

But he was going to turn down Jamison's offer. No doubt about that, either.

Glittering like metal, the skirts of fog wound around the bus, and obscured the storefronts which formed, in a collective vision, a village within a watery cave—the stalactites of mist hanging uncertainly. He thought of the physical dark, not the anxiety, within the hospital, of a corner of darkness where a young man, not three beds from him, had been connected to transfusions, had reddened as he breathed, inhaling and exhaling with ponderous muscular force, as if in defiance of the ward's internal overcast. From the neck down, the muscle is slow in rising, buckling into massiveness, then submission. First the sleek collarbone, vulnerable as he sleeps, the arms resting on either side even though they do not seem to rest; they are pinioned, tense, fixed as if in readiness to give blood, rather than take it. And the shoulders: rounded, rippling planes as a woman's back is rippled, all the way to the waist; and the chest—where there is a sudden swelling on either side with the breathing: veins, clearly visible, part suddenly, with the muscle, pinioned back into the hard curves separating above his heart.

What a great fight the boy had put up. If he could've managed it, he would have broken free, transfusions dragging.

Just to get back into the world. All that muscle, ready to break the apparatus into pieces.

On the street, Tom took his time finding Jamison's house. It was set in back of the Carnegie Free Library, and there was no way of getting to it, except via the path which went around the boarded-up building. Squirrels—and red ivy—were coming at him from all directions, their autumnal heat fighting the fog. The squirrels, muscles bristling, seemed to create a dangerous friction as they skittered across the bark—reminding Tom of "Danger. Do not walk on dry pine needles. Forest fires"—swinging over to the wall of the library, scraping their way across the arms of the dead wrought-iron clock, then down a finger of ivy, the leaves burning after them. Tom looked between the window boards. A hallway of lights was on, a full line of the old police station globes. Probably somebody was sweeping the place. Two flights up: a stained glass window. And at the foot of the stairs: a square of overcast light, and a figure moving within it. The man must have been up on the third floor.

And then Jamison's house, which seemed collared by a moat of November rain. The leaves, floating, made easy rings, but still they formed a consistent fire, reflected in all the puddles, now breaking into slow light as the fog began to burn, disappear.

"Then, what do you want to do?" Jamison would probably ask.

"Just want to sit here and eat breakfast—with you," he'd say.

Once inside, Tom actually said, "I hope I'm not too early."

And Jamison actually said, "No—I've been up and I've already voted. You going to vote?"

"Nope"—sitting down.

"Why not?"

"Too much out of circulation when the issues were coming up."

"I guess it's pretty important—what with Connors challenging the other two." Jamison was trying to talk while tinkering with the last of the breakfast. Very good, considering a man was doing it. Tom was already waiting for Jamison to start his pitch.

"Well?" Tom said, all of a sudden.

Jamison looked over from his kitchenette, which was now receiving the new sun, and seemed to stumble right into the word. Tom's abruptness should have puzzled him, but as it was, he was apprehensive and it showed—that he had been busy with nervous business designs—on Tom. The old man looked hurt, and seemed to say that Tom could have waited, at the very least, until breakfast was over.

"I don't know how heart attacks usually affect people," Tom said, "but it seems to have made me unable to talk to people. So I have to be honest. The fact is, I know you and Karin have been talking—about me. And I know the two of you want me to go back into business, into a partnership with you. But I can't."

The old man put oatmeal in front of him, and asked "Why?"—which Tom wished he hadn't.

"I just can't answer that."

"You're going to have to," Jamison said, "or else I won't let you rest."

Tom smiled. "You're not the plaguing type, Jamison."

"I could be, Jamison said, "especially when there's so much at stake. I don't blame you for shying away from some kind of personal rehabilitation program, but I think you know me well enough to know that I wouldn't stoop to that —not with you. But Compton's is selling out, and I think we could get the rent pretty cheap here in Jutland. Naturally, we wouldn't set the world on fire—but think of it, your own store, run at your own pressure."

"Let's eat breakfast," Tom said.

He thought of the gift specials he could work up, of displays he could build which would crystallize the Norse-Christmas mood of Jutland. "I just can't answer what you've said." And then he wondered about those past moments when he had known the ability to speak both honestly and sensitively, keeping the conscience whole. Now it seemed he had become a seventh-grader all over again, elbowing his way to the truth whenever he could.

"Are you saying there's a chance?" Jamison said.

"No, Jamison, I'm not saying that." Then he wondered if his being secretive was hurting him even more. "What I'm saying is—I can't answer your question unless I'm blunt: no man gets the upper hand of me without me disliking him, and if you and I went into business, you know that's what you would do."

"I don't see how you can say that," Jamison said. "I played stockboy in your sampleroom for months.

"And you bossed me the whole time," Tom said.

"And you resented it?"

"I did."

They spoke no further about it, but behind his eyes, Jamison appeared to be gathering together the last papers of their friendship, in preparation for a closure of the file—"It takes so little," Tom decided. On their way to the men's club meeting, they spoke hardly at all, Tom hoping there would be enough jokes from the crowd to break this deep ice. There were a few, but then Tom found himself making a few ill-timed comments, in front of the audience. When they were out on the sidewalk, Jamison said, "Hell, what's the matter with you?"

"Nothing," Tom said, opening the hotel door for him. They were out on Third Avenue.

"Then why did you ask something like that?"

"Because I don't think any of us knows what it's like to be in Vietnam."

They came to an intersection. They wanted to separate. "I'm sorry," Tom said, "about this morning—I mean earlier this morning. I was hoping I could make you see what I was saying."

"No"—still bitter—"I think I do."

"No, I think you don't. But let's try to let it go, if we can."

"I just can't get over it," Jamison said, "why you'd lay your life down almost for a man like Webb, and then when it comes to me—"

"If I had it to do all over again, that's not what I would have done. Maybe I'm paying the consequences for it now. Anyway, I can't let that push us into a partnership which I know we couldn't finish."

Jamison shook his head. "O.K., let's say I'm trying to understand. And maybe we can get together again—sometime." He was afraid of mentioning the club.

"Sure, I'll give you a call."

They separated with a handshake, but Tom still sensed a resistance.

NINE

He walked on over to First Avenue, then down a block to Wymansales, looking all the way up to the eighth floor. Fullerton, the new man from St. Louis, was probably up there, getting things in line.

Down First Avenue, in the direction of the trainyards and the moment when the street becomes the classic skid row. The usual resident-tourists, ransacking the Salvation Army stores; the salesclerks standing at their gilt windows, frightening off the browsing public. And with this, the smell of the waterfront—cockles and garbage liè at the base of the street, feeding the seaweed glitter of the arcades and pornography stands—and the crash and rhythm, the sea's, a prologue to the rhythm of the brickstone trainyards, and the SHOWBOX THEATER, closed down, fenced in with boards hiding the old posters, the displays of the thirties and forties—like those in WEBB'S—WE'VE GOT IT—WEBB'S. And he saw the caboose again, and the store, the entrance, on opening day after they'd moved in the stock, after they'd hauled in the load from the florist, when they'd done up the place, cut the ribbon, and let the OPENING SALE people in, when they'd turned on the branching neon in the later afternoon—WEBB'S—WEST GREEN—Sale entire stock of $5.00—$3.95—the cardboard silhouettes in the back—bellhops—described, in his own handwriting, as "Effective Backgrounds of Felt Appliqué on Color—White Shoes Displayed on Black Bases, Black shoes on White with Drape-Drop Curtains."

SHOWBOX THEATER. He wondered how Ed was. Whether he was coming home soon.

"I used to always go to this black shoeshine man," a remembered voice said, "and he had this kind of split store—or corner of a building—which he part-owned with this white tailor. And they hardly ever said anything to each other, not because they had a grudge, but just because one had his work and the other had his. Anyway, I used to go to both of them, and one day, when I went there to pick up my pants, the shoeshine hall is locked up. When I asked the tailor, 'What's the matter?' he said that he'd come in the week before, just after he had been on a week's vacation. And there the place was—all locked up.

"After asking around, the tailor found out that it'd been locked up almost during the whole time he'd been on vacation. So down First he goes, to the partner's hotel, which is not all that far from his own—and there inside his room he finds his partner dead over a week."

He went down to Carsteer's Health Club and was allowed in—on an extended guest pass. It was noon, and the place was crowded.

"Hey, Mr. Hill," Barney said, "I hear you've been sick. How about a massage?"

"Not today," Tom said, taking off his clothes. "I just want to sweat."

He opened the door at the back of the locker room and found only a few men sitting there, naked in the fog. They seemed to be homosexual, and when they saw his body clearly, they withdrew, staring at their knees. Tom smiled, thinking for the first time that people must be seeing him as a wreck. "Wreck" was such a good way of putting it—like the word "tart"—given to a woman.

The men were cowering under the steam.

One said, "How many laps you do?"

"Fifteen. How many did you do?"

"Sixteen."

"I'll tell you what," the first said. "For every pound that I outweigh you, I'll have to do an extra lap. And for every pound that you outweigh me, you'll have to do an extra lap."

Others were coming in—also men of business. Some were

from the club. Including Jim Sandberg—and an up-and-coming real estate broker, Torgrimson.

"Hello, Jim," Tom said, gazing up but still leaning against the wood.

"Hello." The broad-chested patriarch snubbed him by sitting in a far corner; gradually a shield of sweat broke out upon a sterling-silver chest.

"That was a very unfortunate thing you said today, Tom."

"Right—I guess."

Sandberg looked at Torgrimson. Righteously askew. "I guess you're not going to apologize?"

"Does that father—Jim Hant—think I should apologize?"

"What do you think?"

"If that's so," Tom said, really thinking about it, "then I will, but I don't think it'll help."

"Why won't it?"

Tom looked at him. "What do you think?"

Sandberg bending as the steam relaxed him. "You'd like this country to claim responsibility for his son's death, wouldn't you?"

"That's what I was asking him," Tom said.

"That's pretty revolutionary," Torgrimson said. "Who revolutionized you?"

"You a father?"

"Yes."

"Of a son?"

"No."

"I thought so," Tom said, "and neither is Jim here."

Torgrimson nodded sympathetically. "I see what you mean. Ella's brother was killed, but I still don't know what it would have been like—if he'd been my son. He was killed," he said, looking up and appearing almost confessional, "almost the same time she was—to the day."

Sandberg had become unnerved, as well as depleted by the steam. "That's not the point, though. How do you think we feel—Tom—standing judgment month by month on literally hundreds of draft-board cases? How do you think I feel when the students on my own campus get hurt and even maimed because we don't understand each other?"

Tom watched him, his silver chest and hair—laurelled, aristocratically, by wisps of steam. It was impossible for him to tell if this was just another orchestration. "I can't answer that because I don't know how you feel."

Sandberg settled back, content, seemingly, that his point had been made. "So your son's up for Pre-Induction?"—taking a risk.

"That's right," Tom said.

"You know the Physical doesn't always mean Induction."

"I know what it means," Tom said. He got up and went into a cold shower. Still, it was impossible to say if Sandberg had been speaking sympathetically. And Torgrimson—had been on the compassionate side of the fence all along. Through what? He remembered the write-up—unintentionally facetious—of Ella's—the wife's—"tragedy." And so if Torgrimson had a daughter, he had to pour out her milk every morning at the breakfast table—which meant he could understand, as stand-in mother, why all parents wanted their sons out of Da Nang.

He rubbed his slackened muscles hard, dried off. Out on the street again, he headed directly for Cicero's. Smell of leather as he went inside. It had been so long since he'd been near shoes that he could actually notice it, now. Kernan was at the back of the place, busy talking with Gene Aldridge, manager of Cicero's chief opponent—The Clothes Line, across the street. Tom wondered what in the world Kernan was doing, talking with him. The Clothes Line had been notorious for tapping other outfits for information, as well as robbing them of their top-notch salesmen.

"Tom Hill," Clothes Line said, "hear you've been sick."

"Good to see you," Kernan said, shaking hands. "What can I do for you?"

Clothes Line was doing too much watching. "Look, I didn't mean to interrupt," Tom said. "Why don't you two go ahead and finish what you were talking about. I'd just like to have a minute with you, Kernan, when you're through."

Jamie came back from lunch.

"What you say we talk about it while we're eating," Kernan said.

"I've already eaten, thanks," Tom said. He was working hard against the invitation. "Besides, lunch hours are for men who work." The other men were silent. "I actually came here, Kernan, to see if you had any work open."

"Well, Tom, not just now"—Tom started helping him out with nods even before he'd finished. "I do have Jamie here"—a thug version of Sal Mineo, 1959—" and two others part-time, but—"

"Christopherson's might need somebody," Clothes Line said, unexpectedly.

"Hey—yeah—I'd think you'd have a good chance there."

"Yeah—I'll try it"—trying to swallow "chance."

The three of them walked out together. "If nothing else turns up," Kernan said, turning, "give me a call. I'm sure I can locate somebody."

"Thanks again." And shook hands, even with Clothes Line. He watched them go up First, to the Cavalier Broiler. Steak sandwich with salad and Roquefort dressing, $1.95. He wondered how long it would be before Jamie got good enough for Clothes Line to grab. Maybe another two months. He couldn't wait that long. Not with Karin hysterically restoring the house every moment that he was home. He became aware that he was wandering—also resentful that Kernan indirectly favored a punk over him. He would just love to have Clothes Line try to get him to defect, *if* Kernan ever hired him.

He was still wandering—half-laughing at the fact that this was some great crisis for him. It would have been a year ago. He wondered how he would have managed a choice between convalescent oblivion and the will to pound the pavement. Under the old laws. One half of the choice would have seemed so evil he would have been momentarily frozen—even by the thought that immobility could have been attractive.

So Kernan favored a punk and flaming asshole. Well, maybe a punk and flaming asshole were best for the world of mobility. And maturity. And remember: he'd just dumped Jamison, the best man on earth, into the trash, when for all intents and purposes, he'd handed his job and health on a platter to Samuel Webb—"Webb (We've Got It) Webb," who most certainly was not worth the powder to blow his brains out and who, after a limited period of sodden mourning, had gone back to the farm. So the rumor went.

At the bus stop, his conscience—he could tell—was busying making a big either/or out of it. Stay here and job search or go back home. And either way, he'd be bitched—by being too submissive one way or aggressive the other: either the milquetoast or the silly martyred hero.

He took the first bus that came—neither bound for the deeper city center of jobs nor bound for home, either. Between the either/or. When he felt like it, he got off. He was in the middle of the Kelly District, south of Jutland. He walked into a store.

"Looking for work—any kind, any hours, any pay."

"Nope—sorry—try the Cat and Canary across the street."

"Looking for work, any kind, any hours, any pay."

"Are you kidding? But good luck."

"Looking for work, any kind, any hours, any pay."

"Full up until Christmas. Try us then."

"Looking for work, any kind, any hours, any pay."

"Sorry, but we are taking on trainees. Would you consider?"

"I need it now. Right this minute. Looking for work, any kind, any hours, any pay."

"Now? Afraid not."

"Looking for work—"

He'd finally hit a manager with enough irony. Chad of Chad's. Chad tossed him a quarter. "O.K., go get us both some coffee."

"Looking for work—not slave labor—any kind, any hours, any pay."

Chad tossed him his dust rag—also Windex. "How's that?"

"That's better."

Chad sat him down, asked him a few questions. "You know I am looking for somebody"—he wasn't given to tact—"an old guy—to sell this trash part-time."

The bus back home. Fifteen hours a week would not save their house—there was no doubt now, they'd have to sell it—but the work input was still there. A token? He tried to trace the currents of the day—Jamison, refusal of Jamison, the club, rejection of club (which was mutual), Wymansales, First Avenue, Showbox, Carstair's, Kernan and Clothes Line, and then the bus. What had moved him from one spot to the next? Still he said, "Name it, name it, name it," and still he was saying, "I can't answer that."

When he got home, Karin would say, "Well, are you and Jamison in business?" And he'd say, "No—but look what I've got in the way of a token."

A token. A token wouldn't keep a house like theirs—the unemployment insurance wasn't that much. A token wouldn't keep a son in Stanford, or any school for that matter.

"Sorry, this is what I've got, and this is what I'm going to offer. A token. A gesture."

And Karin would say, "What's the use of a gesture?" And she would turn against him, thinking that he'd turned against himself—permanently. And maybe that was the case, but he still couldn't rebuild himself back into what he had been. Just as it had been impossible for him not to go to St. Louis, so it was impossible, now, to send out his commitments again.

But still this token. "Hey, Karin, I've got this token."

"Fuck your token."

"Fuck my token."

"This bus," the boy on the bus was saying, "boy, do I hate buses."

"Yeah," his friend said, "they make me sick. Nauseous."

"Nauseated."

"Nauseous."

The bus was almost empty, so the driver had heard.

"How'd you like to drive one all day, buddy?"

"I'd sure hate that," the boy said.

"Oh, I sure like drivin'," the bus driver said, cutting him off—

> "In my big black Buick '59
> Oh, you know, the ridin's mighty fine
> In my big black Buick '59."

The boy, put off, turned to his friend. "Read about another hijacking."

"Yeah?"

A nod—as if it had been inside information. "And the woman with the gun had two grenades in her bra." Still deadpan.

Tom and the driver laughed.

"Well?" the boy asked soberly. "How'd you like it if you were on the plane?"

"Were you on it?" Tom asked.

"No—but still."

"Some guy'd probably come up and try to give her a little feel and get his hand blown off," the driver said. ". . . Ah, shit"—seeing a passenger at the next stop. "Ah, she-et. I wanna go home:

> "In my big black Buick '59
> Oh you know, the ridin's mighty fine
> In my big black Buick '59."

"It's a good idea," somebody else said. "Wearing grenades in your bra. Specially these days. They never caught that maniac."

"They should go running after those guys who try that stuff."

"Some guy try that with my wife," the boy said, "I'd go running after him all right—find out why he had such bad taste."

"My wife," the bus driver said, "doesn't need to wear grenades in her bra. She's thoroughly protected by her face."
He slowed. Two more got off.

"Oh, I love drivin' in my big black Buick '59.
Oh, the ridin's mighty fine in my big black Buick '59."

"This guy's a real swinger," the boy said, "he's just learnin' how to comb his hair like Elvis. Up with the times."

"Man," the driver said, checking the mirror for mixed company, "having some hair to comb is better than no hair at all. And you know where I mean."

"Oh, gees, I don't," the boy said.

"You sweet little blossom, you," the driver said. "I bet you and your friend there make out mighty fine."

"Ecstasy comin' and goin' all the way," the friend said. "It's better than an ugly wife."

"Oh, I love drivin' in my big black Buick '59.
Oh, the ridin's mighty fine in my big black Buick, '59."

A woman got on. Hair style: Barbara Stanwyck, 1941. Shoes: pointed, 1956. Corinna pattern.

"I had this hag, see," a remembered voice said. "God, what a hag! Well, anyway, we had our big year-end-sale, crowded as hell, even had the racks up, the wooden racks. Well, anyway, we were just nuts enough to put the Corrina pattern on sale: $3.49."

"You were nuts," Tom answered.

"I was nuts—or we were nuts. Well, anyway, this woman puts them on and they fit like a dream. And so I say, 'Should I wrap them up, Lady?' And she says, turning around and around in the mirror, 'Well, I don't know—they're a little pointy.' 'Well, that's O.K., Lady,' I say, 'Wear 'em on your head.' But she was a little slow getting the idea of pointed shoes, pointed head. All she does is still turn around and around in the mirror, 'I see what you mean,' she says, 'but that's still a lot of money,' she says, 'to pay for shoes that are so pointy.' Holy shit! She probably would have worn 'em on her head, if I'd dropped the price by half a dollar."

> "Oh I love drivin' in my big black Buick '59
> Oh the ridin's mighty fine in my big black Buick
> '59."

"It's winter," Tom thought, looking through the window.

The woman with the forties' hair was looking at him. "Tom Hill," she said.

Tom blinked. "I'm sorry—"

"Sally Myers," she said. "Used to be on switchboard at Wymansales. I was there for just a couple of months."

"Sure," Tom said, actually recalling her, "I remember." It felt good, remembering her.

"What're you doing now?" she asked.

"Selling clothes and shoes—part-time. How about you?"

"I work the counter, down at Kress's."

"How do you like it?"

She shrugged. "How about you?"

"I just got put on today," Tom said. "I'll have to wait and see."

"Jobs sure come and go fast," she said, "don't they?"

"Yes, Mam, they do."

"Well, Mr. Hill, here's where I get off. Sure glad I saw you again."

"Sure glad I saw you."

"Ah she-et," the driver said, having to slow down.

Tom watched her through the window. Then the lamps, encircled with the angel-hair of mist and smog. Only six-thirty and they were all on. Smell, now, of Sail tobacco—and the last odor of burning peat. The bus billboard: "Isn't it good to know that every day a Holiday Inn is being opened?"

The bus driver was making accusations that the boy had no balls.

"It's better having no balls," the boy said, forcing it, "than having them lop-sided."

"Jesus Christ," Tom thought, "do I feel good. Holy shit, do I feel good."

And Ed, sitting in the locked room, was already being taken back to a decade earlier—virtually two decades—and he was left with random points of conversation, different in tones and assumptions from anything which could be spoken now.

It was as if he could go back, touch the family Packard when it was new and see age in everything that was fresh; as if he could file back through the signatures of Life *magazine, turn to the ad for the '57 Packard and see that it was old because it looked new—and he saw his father in his shirt sleeves, out in the fields of the Webbs' farm, and he kept saying, "So you think chickens'll come home to roost?"*

The runner was at the starting line.

They were standing close to the carnival.

"What's that sound?"

"What?"

"The song—what's it called?"

They stood very still. The ferris wheel turned again. It was raining.

"Yes. 'I Get the Blues When It Rains/I Can Never Lose When It Rains.' "

And in the locked room, he heard other songs, "At Last," "Donkey Serenade," "So Long, It's Been Good to Know Ya," "Wheel of Fortune," "I Wanna Love You," which were all there, in his father's voice.

Sunday. Ed goes out running on the campus.

The question—#4—had read, 'Have you ever given expression publicly or privately, written or oral, to the views herein expressed as the basis for your claim?"

The runner was at the starting line, waiting for the second hand to come back around. A tightening in the fingers. Sweat. The reserve of energy rocks tentatively; settles at the base of the spine. Contracts into a shield, straining. His arms slightly forward, rigid, like the twists in oak boughs.

Ed had written, "Yes, I have participated in a demonstration designed as protest against the manufacture of—"

He had stopped writing.

And now in the locked room,

Sunday. Ed goes out swimming.

he asked why he kept blocking it out. It was morning—almost nine o'clock. The milling crowd was pushing him forward. Thinking of his father, he had not resisted. He had seen the patrol car coming, and was now ready to meet them. Receptive.

The starting gun goes off. Hard the first lap, total self-indulgence, hurtling along one chord of the track, exultant as he nearly tilts off. Going past the first of the finish lines, he thinks, "No tone, too fast." And the legs and neck cords are tight, overwrought with the shock of the first lap and the despairing sound of the lungs, running ahead of themselves, against themselves: second lap.

And the next two laps. Hoping they will blur. They do. The speed of the air is cooling, drying. Then it hits the lungs. A rasp—goes deeper than he thought. The chest toughens against the strain, and momentarily he sees his competitor—taut, swift, biceps flexing with the rock of arms. Diffusion, and the chest constricts. He can taste dryness; the incessancy of his speed and the counterpoise of his lungs give the atmosphere a friction: "going for two more," another finish line, "going for one," and now the competitor pulling ahead, with the double pulse pressing up cruelly against the plate of muscle—and—

Ed goes out running. His friend Robb surmounts the hill, while Ed starts the climb, fighting dust, leaves, and last year's asthma. Coming to the top, he feels his lungs sink as the distant track bowls beneath him, two men pacing along the great ellipse of grass, ready to use the next white line as the starting point; suddenly Robb begins circling—in hot pursuit of the skittering refinement of flesh and bone, his eyes set on the rhythmic back which seems to defy all laws of energy. Ed reaches the starting line, his breath exultant for 45, 50, 90 yards. Another line wings past; he reaches Robb and their breathing joins, diastole, systole, in a brotherly conspiracy to murder, enslave the enemy 45 yards ahead; Ed feels the thong of muscle tighten across his chest, sees the shellacked radiance of Robb's body, the easy harmony of his pacing, anticipates, for a second, his own victory, and instantly a rasp enters his lungs—

The crowd—he allowed it to—edged him close to the patrolman.

Forcing himself ahead, he feels his stomach constrict, close in; his lungs, teasing suffocation, clamp tight, and entering the critical chord of the track

he deliberately elbows the patrolman, and the nightstick comes down

blackness rims his sight

a magnificent surrender! One stroke! Another, as he falls, aware of the confusion of his senses.

Sunday. Ed goes out swimming. He follows the other man

slowly, entering a lake which is now a scalding mirror. He first swims easily, nothing between them now but an even wave of water; the white radiance of the shore sets his friend's body to flaming, and he can see, now, the twists of the shoulder muscles, the even scissors of his legs. His own arms lash more firmly, his body rigid, planing and falling —as the man leads him into the core of the lake. And then, as the expanse of water forms a united pressure against his chest, his friend moves ahead.

Ed planes through the water, ignoring his lungs, his legs pushing through the stretches of precisely shaded depth.

"I will arise and go to Jesus"

He fights at his friend, thrusts at his image. His saliva gathers and spills over, his leg muscles loosen and bunch at the same time

"He will embrace me in his arms/In the arms of my dear Saviour—"

But in the locked room and now at the window, Ed sees himself slowing down in the water, becoming calm: not giving in and turning from the naked man and heading in for shore.

And his father was there like a rankling ghost—imminent, threatening, and yet giving him strength.

And he stood up from under the nightstick, clearing a path for himself.

TEN

The Greyhound was pausing at Winton, Oregon. The driver smoked a few more minutes, staring straight through the windshield at the pillars of the town's theater. Ed found himself dozing, dreaming of the erratic dawns and blackouts, which had followed them through the Siskiyous, as the sun had tried to make its way over the mountains.

The driver crushed his cigarette, got up, opening the door. In a moment he had disappeared inside the Winton drugstore. When he returned, he was talking confidentially with a man who was the twin of Bill Haley. They both go on, the stranger bracing himself against the front rail.

"I'll clue you on one thing," the stranger said, "it's worth stopping at. Just ask Ken about his 'firehouse,' and he'll get sore as hell. It's worth it! It's worth it!"

"Wish I could," the driver said, dreamily smoking again, "but you know it's three o'clock—Seattle."

"You going to make it what with the squalls and all?"

"It's not a problem—not now."

They had nothing more to say. The friend looked dumb, leaning there.

"Yeah."

"Yeah."

And then, without another word, the man was gone. The driver went on looking at Winton—a circle of Hoovervilles of clapboard and ice, mercifully deserted, and boarded up with sheets of buckling plywood. And now people were waking up, wondering and talking about the delay—just as the driver crushed out the cigarette and threw the bus into gear. And as the motion started again, Ed fell asleep, dreaming of the sun and the ice splinter of the moon appearing and disappearing above the jagged range of mountains. He awoke at noon, thinking, suddenly, that the ancient woman next to him might have died in her sleep, but he found her awake also, scanning a text with a magnifying glass.

"Who's that you're reading?"

"Ingeman."

Ed tried to make out the print of the text.

"The Danish poet Ingeman," the old woman said, not looking up. For some reason, she was annoyed. There was a delicate strain working in her face, a reflection of civilized pain and intelligence. When she had finished, she said, "Where do you go to school?"

"I used to go to Stanford."

"Do they teach Greek there?"

"Yes."

"I'm delighted to hear that," she said, her hands up. "That's the way I began my education, too."

"But most people don't begin that way," Ed said.

"No?"

Ed hesitated. "They actually begin with Latin."

"Is that the way they started you?" She looked severe.

"Yes."

"And you got honors. I can tell by looking at your face that you got honors."

"No," Ed said, forcing himself. "I flunked."

The word, he could tell, was a shock to the fragile contents of her intelligence.

"Whyever why?"

"That is a good question."

"And one which deserves a good answer," she said, angry.

"I guess," Ed said, smiling, "I didn't put forth the hard work."

"I would think," the woman said, "that could be the only answer." She seemed to wait for some promise that he would try harder next time.

"I'm not going back to school," Ed said, "and so I've got to settle the Army problem."

"Well, the Army life can be a wonderful thing. My husband was a chaplain who was stationed everywhere—Hawaii, Texas, on the Gulf of Mexico—and I wrote some of my best poetry while we were passing from place to place. Especially on the trains. I remember one time when I was coming to meet him at Fall Creek, Iowa, and I was looking out at the stiff joints of the hills just at evening time. It really came to fill me with such a feeling that I simply had to create a poem."

"I know what you mean."

"But we were not always right," she said, suddenly. "We called the Germans terrible Huns and Boche. And whatever did we do? Wilson, our only intellectual President, went over there and tried to establish that League of Nations, and what happened? We broke," she said, pounding her hand, "every one of those articles. And so you know now, why Hitler came into power. The Germans, my dear, were a humiliated race, and they were looking for someone to come and heal their wounds. A Messiah, if you want to put it that way."

She leaned back, a small woman, perhaps ninety years old. As she rested, the strain returned to her face, the latticework. Ed was intimidated by her civilization and was glad she slept.

Men were shaking out their topcoats with the arrival of the city's outskirts. Deep smell of sweat. Outside, the stands advertising cream and fresh brown eggs. Motels that were perfect "L's" in the distance, separated from the road by planes of land, scraped clear of all brush and evergreens. The gateways of the train trestles, cobwebbed with iron fencing; the pottery stands, gigantic now with the acres of flamingoes and trolls, all seeming to belong to one enormous bathrom shelf; the trainyards, hidden from sight by a density of four-tier telephone lines; the bell-fronts of the hotels painted the color of ground coffee; the discarded rivers disappearing behind the lunch counters, the color of molten metal. The slum sales buildings, with their constant angelic horizons dawning on the front.

He was watching the traffic funnel up Fourth Avenue, when he happened to catch sight of his Uncle Marl. He was sure that he had just come from Carstairs Display, picking up something for his Jutland Dimestore. He wondered if the ancient woman sleeping next to him would have been scandalized by an introduction. Ed felt defensive. Marl was the hub of Jutland, and in being the hub of Jutland, he was the hub of Seattle. Ed tried to signal him but missed his chance.

They were arriving at the terminal. Taking down his thin jacket, he got the woman's carryall and galoshes.

"Oh, yes," she said, snapping forward. "There was something in Ingeman which I wanted you to see."

The people were already up, crowding one another.

"Yes—"

It was a poem which had to do with a sunset and a castle.

"Yes," Ed said, irritated. He returned the book and started, somewhat hesitantly, to enter the crowd. She didn't seem to care.

Outside, he grabbed his luggage and turned in the direction of the Federal Building, but a moment later, he saw her getting off the bus, looking blind and frightened.

"Do you have someone picking you up?" he said, coming back.

"Yes, my Ernest will be here."

Ed wanted to remind her her husband was dead.

"Look," he said, "where do you live?"

"Jutland."

"Jutland—fine—we can take the bus together."

'That's fine," she said absently, "and I'm sure you'll take Greek once you're finished with Latin."

"Yes—" he said, taking up her baggage. Once they were on the bus line, they had to transfer twice. He got her to Jutland's central avenue.

"My building, my dear," she said, pointing across the street. In back was the old Jutland library, long since abandoned and put up for sale. No one would touch it—its central room, the stacks, was one continuous copper-green spiral, disappearing into a canopy of skylights which no janitor had had the nerve to clean. Outside, the dead hands of the wrought iron clock had become white with the droppings of pigeons.

"My dear," she said, "we shall take the elevator. It would be wrong to reject these changes."

The elevator was the kind which had an inner and outer door. Ed pressed the button for her. His back was tired from their combined luggage.

"It's remarkable that such a young man as you would take me all the way here. I simply can't believe," she said, "that you flunked Latin."

"Oh, you'd be surprised," Ed said, angry. "People of limited capacity can often be polite."

They came to the end of the rosette hall. To his shock, she was knocking at the door of her own apartment. It opened —to Ed's surprise and fury, Ernest lived.

"My dear, here is a young man who was good enough to be porter to my luggage." She turned to him. "This is my nephew."

"Thank you," the old man said. "Caroline, you're a day early." He was pulling the luggage inside. "Please, sir, let me do it. I can do it. Caroline, you've made a mistake. And you should've called me."

"Very true, I have," she said. "And I've caused this young man so much inconvenience. Please leave your name and phone number and we'll invite you over for Christmas cake." She was already sitting at her letter desk, mixing old papers with new ones from her purse. In back of her was a wooden screen, a walnut lacework of calla lilies and black birds, through which a storm of dust and sunlight passed, mute and ceaseless. She was not even looking at him.

Ed went out without answering and the nephew followed him into the overheated hall.

"I'd like to shake your hand again," he said. "Thank you."

"It was easy," Ed said, moody. He couldn't get at the bottom of his anger.

"Please come back again," the nephew said. "It sure

would be good to get some conversation." Momentarily Ed understood him to mean that the old woman disregarded him as well. But he said, "I'd like to say yes but I can't be sure. Nice to have met you." He disengaged his hand and took the elevator downstairs. He had gone far out of his way, but he could still get to his draft board before it closed. Another bus took him to the city center, and from there he had only four blocks to walk.

"Yes, sir," the clerk said, once he had set down his luggage. She was the beautiful woman he remembered—in her late fifties.

"I'd like to find out," Ed said, "if I can apply to be a Conscientious Objector."

"Let me have your card," she said, "and we can find out." She checked his number and got his file.

"You are classified I-A?" she asked, smiling.

"Yes—I got the card last week."

"And you're up for a Pre-Induction Physical?"

"Yes."

Ed, still angry with the first old woman, was annoyed by the obvious questions. It was as if she were testing to see if he would return civility for civility.

"You understand, then, that you have 30 days in which to request a personal appearance and/or appeal?"

"I do now."

Her gaze wandered a little, offset by his change in tone. "We can really make no decision as to your draft status until we see how you fare physically. But if you fill out Form 150 now, and request a personal appearance, the Board could probably act on everything later this month. How does that sound?"

Ed, watching her look up at him, felt she was testing for civility again. He could picture her as a faculty wife, arranging her husband's students in a half-moon around the fireside, feeding them stove-popped popcorn and listening for mistakes.

"It sounds all right," Ed said, "if I can get the Form 150

done in time. I've been working on a copy of the questions ever since I've been at school, and they're not easy to answer."

"Be that as it may," she said, angry at his lack of gratitude, "I'll get you the form." She made him believe, now, that he was causing her a great deal of bureaucratic trouble. But Ed, remembering the other woman, would not allow himself to sound solicitous.

She dated the form and handed it across, placing the burden of conversation on him.

"What are the new policies on religion?" Ed asked, paging through, "in order to score well on this?"

"Religion is of the essence," she said, trying to shock him with her vocabulary, "of the very essence. You must think through your answer very carefully and be sure to include a letter from your minister, if you have one."

Ed's anger floated to the top of his thoughts. "I have been thinking it through. It's one of the reasons I flunked out." He found he could say nothing more—she was only staring at him. "Thank you," he said, feeling ludicrous, and turned away.

He stopped at a corner and found, with the shame behind, that he was afraid to go home. His decision to submit the form and thereby complicate matters could prove to be the last straw on the great pack of his father's problems. He returned to Jutland again, and got off at the center of Market Avenue.

His uncle didn't seem surprised to see him. Only happy. "Your mother's getting anxious to see you," Marl said, putting an arm around his shoulder and steering him toward the lunch counter. "We've all been anxious, in fact."

"I thought I'd just stop in," Ed said, "since I was in the district anyway."

"When you come here," Marl said, "you don't have to have a reason."

Ed was quiet. They were at the counter. "Marl, I've decided to go C.O., even though I might get a deferment for my asthma. Do you think that's stupid?"

"What's Tom say?" he asked, his brother's name making him shy.

"I haven't talked to him yet," Ed said. "I figured he had enough to worry about."

"That means two years of service, you know—" rapping the counter.

"I realize that, but I don't have all that much to lose. I can't make it at school, so this would be a chance to do something"—he hesitated—"productive."

Marl looked worried, and Ed knew it wasn't the C.O. *per se*. It was the fact that he hadn't told his father.

"Would you like a job here?" Marl asked suddenly.

"Here?" Ed was looking at the merry-go-round which winked Christmas colors at every quarter turn.

"Yes."

"You mean for the holidays?"

"No, I mean indefinitely. It doesn't offer the greatest future—the five-and-dime—but it could keep you in business for awhile."

"I couldn't," Ed said. "It'd be too easy."

Marl misunderstood—deliberately. "So you think it's easy? I'd work you enough so you'd change your tune. Easy," he whispered.

"I don't mean the job, I mean a job under my uncle."

"You're just like Tom used to be. Proud. To the hilt. Making the worst for yourself. O.K. Go ahead, make the worst for yourself, but maybe someday you'll understand you can make a lot of people happy by doing the best for yourself."

Ed was watching him, tracing out his father's features. "You said Dad used to be that way."

"Don't ask me, Ed, any more than I think it's right to tell you. Your father's changed. The rest you'll have to learn for yourself. I want—" he said, standing up and reaching into the glass case, "for you to try some of this mince pie."

Ed finished his coffee and had some. Marl was relieved. "I don't want to keep you from your work," Ed said, pushing his plate away. "And I've got to get on home."

"I understand," Marl said.

"I really appreciate," Ed said, shaking hands, "being able to tell you all this."

"You're going to go C.O., then?"

"I think so—it would be two years well spent."

"What about waiting until you know if you've passed the physical?"

"If I'm C.O. now," Ed said, realizing he was fulfilling Marl's image of his father, "I should let my board know that's the way I think."

"Whatever you decide, you always have a job here when you want it."

"Thanks." Ed felt himself wanting to linger, but he knew home must come, eventually.

Outside, the district was closing up. A Tuesday night, with the mountains flaming just beyond the old library, great chunks of radium. The noiseless bells swung from the wires, doubled back on themselves when the wind got heavy. Ed, getting on the bus, kept thinking of the old woman who had sat beside him.

"I have to get on over to the Federal Building," he had told her.

"Yes"—perfect knowledge, perfect ignorance—she had answered.

And he looked at the driver. No different from the man who had taken them up from California. And the people. Was there any way of telling that they were Seattle men and women, coming home for work, instead of Greyhound transients, riding up from San Francisco.

They were driving down Jutland Avenue, its signs as bright as sky-writing, flamed by a sunset. The newsstands were all abandoned now, their papers blowing submissively under dark-orange bricks. The district went back to World War I, returned to World War II, then degenerated into random Victorian housing for at least two full blocks. The glass in some of the windows was stained—wreaths draped around crests, ships standing in washed-out harbors. Together the panes formed a collage: a pier town somewhere, full of fishwives and dock workers. The sky was usually overcast, except in the late afternoon, when the shops along the boardwalk folded, and everyone went home, watching the clouds that were orange crystals.

The bus crossed a bridge; the canal opened beneath, the moored gas station advertising Texaco for the small craft. The smokestacks smoked out their ironish blue, creating a latticework of pollution and color. The lattice collapsed, took fire as it reached the coals of the mountains. The smokestacks turned on their lights for the low-flying planes. For a second, the evening city was reflected perfectly in the toiling bay. The bus turned off the main road, and they were entering his parents' district. Ed signalled to get off.

He could see his house clearly, but it was another block before he saw that it had been put up for sale. A defeated house—and no one had turned on the lights. Across the gorge, the roundhouse took in another train; and a few blocks further, a car drove up to the corner market.

A defeated house. The rockery had gone to seed; it had seen October and November without a cutting. His sunflowers had been allowed to collapse and rot. He thought of all the houses on his paper route where you had to part the grass in order to reach the porch.

The place was locked up. He went out to the garage and got the key. Stacks of shingles and kindling. No car. Returning, he opened the door and—he saw that it was a house built in the 1930's. He had never noticed. They had a breakfast nook with two leaded windows; a sink bordered with striped tile; a gangling faucet with a raw mouth; a snap-door cooler, built right into the wall; and the universal confetti linoleum.

He stopped in the unlit kitchen and smelled the house. And the dining room dark because of the leaded glass and the Venetian blinds. Above the table: a five-bulb chandelier, wired to the ceiling. All the chairs had been pulled back to the wall, as if his father and mother had not eaten there since he'd left. The piano: closed, covered with stacks of mail.

Resting on the couch, Ed checked the time—nearly six. The furnace snapped off. Night came into the living room. Then he began to hear the breathing.

Not heavy breathing, but resigned. The kind that bides its time. His father's. Ed went to the bedroom door and watched. His father, fully dressed, lay on the bed with his arms behind him. He had never known his father to sleep with his clothes on, had never known him, in fact, to sleep in the early evening. All the rigidity had gone out of his face —which was good—but Ed could see nothing of the earlier strength. Only humor. The glib posture frightened him.

In the breakfast nook, he turned on the light. Seeing his own reflection, he felt his beard, sniffed his clothes. He showered and changed, then sat in his old room. Still that breathing.

Then he heard her car. He ran to the breakfast nook, snapped on the garage light. That seemed to tell her. She saw him through the window.

"It's so good having you back. You don't know."

She had come running from the garage, but it wasn't until she hugged him that he realized he was supposed to make up for a deficit. He shied away, sitting down at the breakfast table.

"How's Dad?" he said.

"Why he's fine. He has a job—two jobs." She opened the refrigerator and put away some groceries.

"What in?"

"A clothing store—and the Terence Fieldhouse."

"Really? Doing what?"

"He helps kids make model airplanes."

Ed looked at her, shocked. She had not anticipated it, but now she realized, seemingly for the first time, how flat the job sounded. She stood at the refrigerator, still holding the door open. "Dad's doing all right," she said, "but as you've already seen, we're having to sell the house."

"Where are we going to live?" Ed asked.

"In an apartment," she said, consciously matter-of-fact.

The consciousness bothered him. He didn't know what to say. At first he thought of insisting that he could bring in a little money, but then he remembered—Pre-Induction. He hadn't told her.

"How long are you on vacation?" she asked, searching.

"—three weeks," he said, wanting to tell her.

"Did your grades work out all right?" she asked.

"No," he said, flatly. "I'm dropping out of school."

She was still putting away groceries. A garbage truck pulled up to the house. He anticipated her next question. "I am up for a Pre-Induction Physical with the draft," he said, "but I've also got the papers here for a C.O."

"You mean they've classified you that already?"

"No—I have to apply for it, and then go see them. Sometime later this month."

The garbage men were walking back down the driveway, the cans slung over their shoulders.

"You mean you could be drafted?"

"Not for a couple of months."

She went to the sink and leaned. Ed understood that while he had always visualized himself as being his father's great second chance, it was really his mother who had made the romantic investment.

"Let's say," she said, "you get the C.O. What then?"

"I'll go right away into alternative service. Usually it's not too bad. And sometimes you can do some good."

The garbage men came back with the empty cans. They picked up some old laurel cuttings and a couple of cardboard boxes of compost. Ed turned on the porch light to help them. They signalled on their way back down. The truck drove away.

"You may as well know," she said, coming into the room and sitting opposite him, "that Dad has changed."

"That's what Shirley and Marl said. Why has he changed?"

"I don't know," she said, "but it's become almost unbearable at times to see him the way he is."

She was clearly aware of her evasion, and for a moment she enjoyed the suspense—even in view of what it was costing him. But then she said, "He's become . . . casual. He doesn't mind things anymore."

"What's wrong with that?" Ed asked, angry and crestfallen. "I thought it was something terrible."

"I can't explain it," she said, "but the other day the kids in his class wanted to make kites instead of airplanes. So, O.K., fine, all the airplanes are dropped right then and there, and they go in for kite-making. The Director was furious."

"But that's stupid. The kids probably had a great time."

His mother looked betrayed. "But I haven't finished. All the kids stood around and watched, while your father made every last one of them himself."

Ed laughed.

His mother was angry. "Let me tell you something. I drove all the way to Portland thinking he had died, and when I got there he didn't even know me."

"I'm sorry," he said, changed. "I didn't know how it was." But he couldn't help thinking that she was over-dramatizing, romanticizing her suffering.

"There's no way of explaining it," she said, "until you see him yourself. Maybe you two can get away, and maybe," she said, "you can help."

"You mean, reform him?"

"I don't know what I mean," she said. "I'm just glad to have you back, that's all." She kissed him, and got up. "Why don't we go on over to Marty's again and get some steak to celebrate. How long has it been since you last had steak?"

"About three months," Ed said.

But when they got to the market, she spent at least ten minutes comparing prices. Ed kept insisting that they have bacon and eggs, but, no, they were to have steak, of one kind or another.

ELEVEN

Morning—and still his father was sleeping. Ed sat waiting at the kitchen table. His father had slept straight through. The neighboring Jutland chimes played the end of "Christ on the Mount of Olives," at a cumbersome, note-by-note pace, as if each bell had to be sounded by the touch of a wound-up statue. Ed tried to shake himself awake but sensed a resistance. He knew that if he were totally alert, he would become even more nervous about seeing his father. Because he was ready to tell him. He felt sure he could explain why he was leaving school, and still make everything work together.

He waited another two hours. Finally his mother came in saying—as if she were a nurse—"He's up. Why don't you go in?"

When he got to the door, he heard a shade being raised with a violent snatch. Coming in, he saw it flapping like a water wheel. Below, his father was looking at it.

"Ed! Come in! Come in!"

Ed smiled, went up to shake hands, but his father avoided him.

"What a sleep," his father said, slapping his stomach. "Fifteen hours."

"How are you feeling?" Ed asked, sitting on the bed.

"A little crippled, a little crippled. But making out just fine." For the first time in his life, his father took off his clothes in front of him. The skin was loose, resigned, as if melting off the bone. Ed missed the statue-like asceticism.

"I wanted to be up here when you had your attack," Ed said, "but Mom said it was best I stay where I was."

"Sure," his father said slowly, "sure, that was the best thing to do."

Ed kept fighting disbelief. His father's self-possession was completely splintered.

"How'd you get back from Portland?" he asked.

"How?"

"Yes."

His father hesitated, about to step into his pants. "I guess it was by ambulance. We got the bill."

Ed was silent. He was waiting for his father to recognize him. It was a minute before his father broke the pause.

"Well, I guess things are fine with you?"

"No, they're not," Ed said, angry. "I'm not going back to school."

His father, buttoning his shirt, did not look startled. Rather, he gave him a troubling glance which said that leaving school did not make him the world's greatest martyr. Ed didn't like being reminded.

"So you're going to work?"

"Maybe," Ed said, wanting to say more. He feared confession to this Presence, this caricature, but confession was his only means of breaking down the ironical fence, of making him his father again. "I don't know, though," he said, "right now I'm finding it hard to believe in work."

"So am I," his father said, shocking him. "You found any answers yet?"

"No."

"Well, tell me when you do." He turned to the dresser.

"Dad," Ed said, trying a different tact, "I'm going to try for a C.O."

"Wonderful. Good luck with it."

And then he tried talking to his father again and still he couldn't reach him. His father dodged and twisted with every overture, taking him down blind alleys and then leaving him to fend for himself. His father wanted no part of him; he wanted to be left alone, with his vacant ironies.

And Ed went at him again, and his father proved even

quicker. He refused, utterly, to share in his earnestness. "Earnestness," Tom thought. "That's what he wants. I could stand anything but that. Give me a baby whose cynical looks I can stare into, but don't give me a son on the verge of moral problems."

And the fourth time Ed went at him, Tom stopped him cold. There was no sense in leading his son to believe that he could share in these great universal queries; he was beyond them now, and was only left with the technical problem of living out the rest of his life in good taste. For a moment he winced while letting Ed know, but the pain was only momentary and two seconds later he had regained his finesse.

And Ed, frozen, kept thinking about the world of suffering—how it had stopped his father from being the compassionate listener he had remembered. For now he stood watching a man who had moved through and transcended pain, and in doing so, had lost all the attractions which had knit his being together.

And in watching his father, he reached an impasse and was forced to remain silent within himself. But unlike his father, he still found a core of curious magnetism, a center of force. And his greed for conviction still remained.

"What do you think," he said, momentarily suspending their battle, "of going on a short trip while I'm here?"

"What do you want to go on a short trip for?"

"I don't know—we could fish or something. Like we did at Goheen."

"Fish? Do you know what the passes are like?"

"O.K., no fishing then. We could go to Portland or somewhere, just for the hell of it."

"I wouldn't mind," his father said.

But first there was Pre-Induction. At six a.m., his father drove him over to the Federal Building, and from there he was taken, by bus, to the center. After some brief paperwork, he followed the other young men into the locker room. Taking off his clothes, he could understand, once again, why the Army got enlistments. The placards at the post offices said that boot camp was a kind of health spa, where every man was pared down to a muscular essence. It was, in fact, a guarantee of prowess, of an equal footing with the rest of the masculine world.

They were beginning to file out.

"What are your hopes?" someone asked him. The boy was broad and swaggering.

"I don't know," Ed said. "They may knock me out for asthma. How about you?"

"Nothing," the boy said, trying to appear superior in spectacles and underpants, "I'm too goddamn healthy."

They were silent, waiting for the others to get into the X-Ray line.

"Name's Ross," the boy said, shaking hands. Mutual satire.

"So after today, you'll have this whole thing off your mind."

"Maybe."

"I've been doing some draft counseling in the past couple of months, and I know for a fact there are thousands of guys who'd give anything to have your asthma."

"I wish I had it to give," Ed said. He walked in and got his X-Ray.

"Why?" Ross asked, when they were both finished.

"Because even if I get my I-Y, I'm going to apply for a C.O."

"But don't you know asthma is permanent I-Y?"

"I know."

Ross seemed interested. The critical bones of his face made a minute adjustment. As they turned down the hall, his walk became an amble, burdened with a thought. "If I'm inducted," he told Ed, "I'm going to refuse to step forward. I've already sent in my draft card, that's why I'm here."

Ed's face made an adjustment as well. He didn't like acknowledging the boy's moral superiority, but he had to.

Another medic came in and gave new orders. All those who had histories of asthma, heart murmur, and allergies were to step forward. Ed nervously got into line.

"I don't hear anything," the doctor said, once he'd touched Ed's chest with a stethoscope. "You got a letter?"

"Yes."

"Well—get on over into that line."

It led into the office of an older doctor. When he read Ed's papers, he disqualified him, categorically.

On his way back to the locker room, he passed Ross, who gave him a satiric wave from the bench. Opening his locker, Ed guiltily pulled on his clothes. Through the window, the city puffed gently, like a scholar at a pipe, and all the sounds were suddenly like those across an expanse of water. Ed—even with a C.O. interview ahead of him—realized the difference between the way the world looked to him now and the way it was looking for most of the boys in the other room. In future months, he would try, again and again, to make the sympathetic leap, but he could never again reclaim the uncertainty of facing service in Vietnam. He was exiled by his freedom, he told himself—unless, of course, he decided to go for broke and turn in his draft card.

In the next room, he was allowed to hand in his folder early and get on the waiting bus. On the way, he was joined by a few other rejects. They were giddy with their freedom.

"Excuse me, gentlemen," a sergeant said, opening the front door. "After you." He smiled good-humoredly, while they squeezed past. "And that, my friends, is the last time they'll call you gentlemen.'

They laughed. The sergeant laughed, too.

In fifteen minutes they were joined by the I-A's. To Ed's surprise, they did not seem to begrudge them their deferments.

"So," Ross said, sitting down next to him, "you're out and out for good."

"No," Ed persisted, "not necessarily. I don't have to pass the physical to go C.O."

"C.O.," Ross said, near contempt. "C.O."

The bus left them in front of the Federal Building. The moment they were on the street, no one laughed. Instantly everyone understood that it was every man for himself. In silence they all went in their separate directions. Unable to find Ross, Ed crossed the street and went on up to the St. Vargis Hotel. His parents were to pick him up and take him to dinner, hoping, of course, to turn his thoughts away from the examination. He waited in the lobby for half an hour, listening to someone playing "Water Boy." He took a seat where he could watch the pianist through the door of the cocktail lounge, and as he waited, the sun came through the glass entrance, changing the hotel barber shop to a golden cage. Then the clouds, winter ferns, reasserted themselves, and the lobby seemed to close itself off from the street. After a few minutes, he almost dozed, and when he opened his eyes, some bystander had blocked his view with a newspaper: De Gaulle and Vietnam. Ed heard his father's honk and walked out under the arcade.

When he got into the car, he saw that his parents had included a stranger.

"Ed—this is Chad," his mother said. "The man your father works for."

Chad looked a lot like Ross, and Ed didn't take to him. Or maybe he was reading criticism into his features.

His parents were silent, anguished with curiosity, but afraid to come out with the question. Ed wanted to tell them, but Chad's frost-bitten charm held him in check.

"I never found out from Dad," Ed said, "what kind of work he does with you."

Chad winked at his father. "Sort of a rag business, wouldn't you say, Tom?"

"Yeah," his father said, "but maybe we're flattering ourselves calling it that." But he was burdened down, preoccupied. Ed saw that the Pre-Induction had unnerved him.

"I wanted to tell you," Ed said, "I've been disqualified because of my asthma."

His parents relaxed together.

"Congratulations," Chad said. "Glad you won't have to go through what I went through."

"What about the C.O.?" his mother asked. "Does that still stand?"

"Yes," Ed said.

"So," Chad said, "you're going to keep stirring up the snakes, even though you could be finished with them?"

"That's right. Does it make sense?"

"Sure it does," Chad said, "for you."

They were sitting together in the back seat, and Ed knew the reason for the resistance—they were vying for his father.

"I've told Chad quite a lot about you," his father said.

"Everytime he comes in," Chad said, "which, of course, isn't that often."

"What do you mean by that?" Ed asked.

"Simply that your father has a bit part in my store. Right?"

"Right."

"You're lucky to get whatever he's got," Ed said.

"True—although when I first saw him, he came in saying he'd take any hours at any pay."

Ed saw his mother tighten. "Maybe that's the impression your store front gave him—hang loose."

"I'm sure it was," Chad said. "Schlock."

It cancelled out the rest of the conversation. They came to the back of the restaurant. The building was like a magnified chimney, widening into lower floors that were as bright as a furnace. They passed into a vestibule hung with ivy, then beneath the wine-glass of the arcaded dining hall. The rose of the candle-lanterns aged the pillars by a hundred years. Through the windows, cliffs rose above the restaurant; they were topped with a golfing green and stripped madronas, now burning in the glass.

They were waiting to order.

"The other night," Chad said, "I was watching this television commercial—and all of a sudden this guy comes on and says—'Isn't it good to know that every day a new Holiday Inn is opening.' Unbelievable."

His father laughed.

Ed and his mother looked at each other.

"Whenever you get a chance," she said, "you ought to call Jamison Hanshaw—and Mrs. Webb—they've been asking about you a lot."

"Yes, and I want to show you this schoolbook she passed on to me—"

Chad glared.

"What's Jamison doing now?" Ed asked, breaking his thought.

"Nothing," she said, "absolutely nothing. Dad could've gone into business with him, but Dad wouldn't hear of it. A store in Jutland."

"What would you have sold?" Ed asked.

"Rags and trash," his father said—digging—mostly at her. "Like what I'm selling now."

"You've got your point across," his mother said.

"What was my point?" his father asked.

She was silent.

"Do you know what my point was?" his father asked, turning to Chad. Chad let his mouth droop and shook his head.

"You see, there wasn't any point in joining up with Jamison, and that's why I didn't."

"If you had," Ed said, pushing down anger, "I would've thought it was because you liked being your own boss."

Chad glared—with smiles—again.

"Being my own boss," his father said. "I'd sure as hell like to know what that means—particularly in a partnership with Jamison Hanshaw."

"What's wrong with Jamison?" Ed asked, watching his mother.

"Aside from being a nursemaid—nothing. He's flimsy, I've decided. And because I won't agree with him, he won't see me anymore. A nursemaid, from start to finish."

Chad laughed.

"Baloney," Ed said.

"What?" his father said.

"Bullshit," Ed said.

"That's better," Chad said.

Finally the waitress came. Ed fumed while they ordered.

"Eat up," Chad said, "for tomorrow you have your C.O. to worry about—and plan."

"Why don't you shut your hole?" Ed said.

His father was sitting back, delighted.

"And you," Ed said to him, "you don't give a shit about anything, not even Mom, because—you think you've gone through so much. Isn't that it?"

"That's not the reason," his father said, smiling through his ice. "I wish it could be explained that easy."

But his father's face had become taut and strung—a visage was forming beneath the skin. Their eyes united in mutual questioning, and Ed felt, momentarily, that he was being drawn.

TWELVE

At first Tom did not want to take the trip. He kept putting Ed off, saying he wouldn't be able to get a vacation just now. But he knew Chad and the fieldhouse director couldn't care less if he took a week or a year off, and when someone finally came along and bought the house for $15,000, Karin's anger made him want to get away. Besides, she was all for it —maybe Ed could tell him something he didn't know. She packed lunch and dinner, and sent them off with the message that Marl and Ellen were visiting in Portland, too.

For the first hundred miles, Tom didn't say much. For a short stretch, a light snow blew across the road in swatches, and it was difficult to steer. The storm formed a glaring overcast which always promised to break into sun but never turned. It was as if they were driving with time held constant: always ten minutes before sunrise. Tom found himself busy with various defenses of why he had sold the house for so little. He was amazed that he felt the need of defense—it hadn't been so in earlier months.

"What if I told you," Ed said, "that I nearly enlisted in the Army. Would you say I was crazy?"

"No—but why would you want to enlist?"

"To better myself, physically."

" 'The Army builds men'?" He looked over from his driving and smiled.

"Yes," Ed said. "Do you remember my barbells?"

"I sure do," Tom said. "Did you know I used to have them?"

"No," Ed said. "When?"

"When Mom and I were first married, and I was out of

work. It used to make me feel better when I had nothing to do."

"I kept thinking," Ed said, "that if I spent two years building myself up, then I could face this friend of mine and compete with him—man to man."

Tom didn't answer. "But then," he said, finally, "you'd have a war to fight. And you'd find yourself giving in—in more ways than one."

"I didn't think about that at the time."

"I'm glad you finally did. When's your C.O. interview?"

"In three days."

Tom stopped at a toll bridge. "This car," he said. "Does it bother you?"

"No. Why?"

"I was just wondering if our household bothered you. Put together with spit and baling wire."

"No, that doesn't make me uneasy. Not that," Ed said.

"You're older than I thought."

"But now that you've sold the house," Ed said, "you don't have anything to worry about—do you?"

"Yes—financially—I guess we do. What I'm now earning comes to a sum total of $4,000 a year, and that, even combined with the house proceeds won't get us far. They're under contract to pay us $5,000 now and $10,000 later. Quite a lot later. And in bits and pieces. You see," he said, "this was bound to come whether or not I had the heart attack. We were living beyond our means from the start."

"Does it hurt you that it hurts Mom?"

"No. No, I wish I could say it did, but it doesn't. One thing makes me feel good, though."

"What's that?"

"If anything were to happen to me, she'd have all the money she'd need."

It was a long shot, but the tone made Ed ask it. "You mean, you were thinking of killing yourself?"

"Many times," Tom said. "For a while the only thing that held me back was the fact that I probably couldn't get away with it."

"But you were changed."

Tom resisted. "Yes. I kept waiting—but I wasn't satisfied—so now—it's just a matter of watching—"

"That's not good enough," Ed said.

The impasse settled between them again, but with a difference. They both knew it was an impasse. Therefore, the silence was no longer an indifference but an acknowledgement.

They ate their sandwiches without stopping, and the road cleared.

Then—"Trouble up ahead . . ." The car bolted, and Ed saw a man and woman standing beside a half-elevated station wagon. Tom got out, and Ed watched them shaking hands. In a few minutes, he got out and helped with the spare. During a pause, the woman gave them each an orange.

"It's not many who'll stop," she said. "Are you church people?"

"Methodist, I guess," Tom said.

"Well so are we," the man said, squatting by the wheel.

Tom smiled but already he was sweating as he jacked the car to the last notch. Ed tried to take over. "Dad," he said, "you know you're not supposed to."

"You don't mean he's not well?" the woman asked. "Bill get over there and take that."

But his father shrugged them all off and started to examine the flat.

"Well," the woman said, "if I've seen sacrifice, I've seen it now."

Portland arrived a hundred miles later. Ed thought about the man and the woman, how they lived with the crash and breakage of the city. Its lights were organized; its roars followed patterns, like those over an airport; but, still, the noise seemed to exclude wayfaring Methodists who needed aid.

They went by an old courthouse which was being leveled, and its fallen facade stood out like a rainbow after a deluge.

"What a waste," Tom said, not knowing why he said it. He thought of the bronze-striped mail chutes, and the spittoons which were probably in the basement. Marble rubble from the staircase, and stacks of shorthand spirals, taken in the time when court reporters didn't have machines. All of them would be the color of the Yellow Pages.

They checked into a hotel that was two blocks from the train station. Its sides were covered with copper-green anglerfish, and a dragonhead swallowed the base of the marquee's flagpole. Twelve dollars for two beds, two people. They were up high enough so they could see the Columbia.

"This is the way to see Portland," Tom said. "Last time I was here all they would let me see was a wet garden. That hospital was—"

"How about dinner?" Ed asked.

Their phone rang. It was Marl.

"Guess what!" he told Tom. "Ellen's just gotten a part in a play. We came down just on the chance she'd get it."

"You mean she's hit the big time?" Tom said.

"Sure," his brother said, "and she might even give you a couple of free tickets, so you can come and see her."

They named a meeting time for the next night.

"What's she in?" Ed asked, when he was done.

"*King Lear*. I guess she wasn't able to land a part until she came down. I bet, though," he said, "this is as amateur as all get out."

Ed wasn't listening. When he looked up again, he saw his father arranging some glasses.

"Ed, how about a drink?"

Stunned, feeling more Methodist than his father, he said, "You mean liquor?"

His father laughed. "Yes. Liquor." He opened their suitcase and produced a bottle of rye.

"Little water?"

"Yes," Ed said. Feeling unsure, he sat down at the desk. He watched while his father carefully polished the glasses. He then poured an abstemious amount in each, and added a flood of water. He returned, shakily holding the results. He was a very green bartender.

"When I was ten," he said, sitting down, "I was told the things we told you when you were ten. One drink and you're finished. Except that my grandfather—my mother's father—was a great connoisseur of corn liquor and he'd buy it from the poor white who used to live on our place. But with my mother and father being what they were, he used to have to hide it in a feed barrel in the toolshed."

"Did he ever know you were onto him?"

"Not exactly—at least I don't think so. But one day, I was scooping out feed for the chickens and 'clunk'—there was the bottle. And I said to him, 'Look, Grandpa, some drunk's hid his white mule here,' and I smashed it on the floor like nobody's business."

" 'Ah, Tommy,' he says, 'you should'na done that.' Poor Granddad, and with me such a self-righteous brat."

Ed was still worried over his rye. He said, "Why doesn't it bother you to drink anymore?"

"I don't know. Don't ask me—you know what I always hated about raising you?"

"No."

"You were always so goddamn watchful. Mom and I'd tell you one thing, and then we'd go and do the opposite, and pretty soon you'd point it out. I could have strangled you sometimes." He put his glass down. "What do you say we go for a swim?"

"Sure," Ed said. "But where?"

"I know a place."

What? Tom's breath came up in a snatch. The room's arm of shadow clamped him down for a moment. The hotel bed seemed to be moving still, like a car rounding an evening corner. He remembered, precisely, that he had been dreaming of rounding a Jutland corner, that he had seen the neon sign—Bellbuoy Tavern—while all the time he had been seated within that tavern, sipping a glass of beer and pouring more from a pitcher and talking about how dead that

Saturday's business had been; while all the time he had been rounding the corner with the sunset coming through the windshield looking like the molten falls in a foundry, and the smoke from the Jutland lumberyards burning a clear amber in the bluefire of the air. But he was aware, too, waking up at that moment, that he had not been dreaming, simply, of driving past the Bellbuoy but also of eating dinner with Ed in the Smithsonian Dining Room—which they had actually done—of cutting turkey beneath their planetarium dome and thinking about all the other restaurants he had known that had fitted themselves out with amber glass and thinking, "In Jutland there's a gas station which always hangs up a red wreath with a red candle in it at Christmas. In St. Louis, the Vessels Three has a canopy with a fleet of galleons sailing across it. At O'Hare there's a ramp sign which says—"F-Y"—and in Seattle they've closed the Showbox Theater. In Palo Alto the Dutch Oven Cafe makes Welsh rabbit its specialty, and in Brooklyn, just off 50th, you can see a wreath in stained glass, if you lower your head and look under the El, right beside the store with the manger scene behind bars, and the sign, NUDIES NUDIES NUDIES right above it. In Brooklyn there's an Ocean Boulevard, and in San Francisco they call it Ocean Avenue. In McMenton, Oregon, there's a place called The Bell Apartments, boarded up and condemned; while on a Washington ferry, the orange light still burns in the popcorn machine—day and night."

What? Tom became aware of the tremors only as they were beginning to subside. He lay back.

He thought about it during the whole morning and afternoon. But by evening he had almost managed to forget it.

"You're not looking good," Ed said that evening. "You O.K.?"

"Sure," Tom said, resisting. "In fact, I could go for another swim right now."

Ed was silent beneath their umbrella. He sensed the change, and it made him draw in closer. It was just what Tom didn't want.

"We don't have much further to go—another ten blocks."

"I'm still not sure about the walking," Ed said. "Are you sure it isn't too much?"

"I'm all right," Tom said, smiling. "Just see if you can keep up with me."

They met Marl in front of an old vocational school. He seemed to think that his wife was just one step short of the big time, that Vickers Street was just off Broadway. They went into the auditorium, and he sat between them, praising her first from one angle and then from another.

"What part is she playing?" Ed asked.

"Assistant to Goneril or something."

"Is that a big part, Ed?" Tom asked.

Ed waited, hoping Marl would dash in with "yes." Unfortunately, that was the only time he decided not to comment. "It's not a big part—" Ed began.

"But important," Marl said, finally.

"Yes."

The stage lifted its asbestos. There was blue velveteen beneath. Behind, someone was practicing the sound effects which would make the storm. They weren't very formidable, but sounded more like one of the music boxes which Marl sold in his dimestore.

The curtains separated. A poster-paint court and heath. Lattices of foliage provided the rosemary for Edmund, the cuckoo flowers for Lear. Ellen made a good attendant to Goneril, but it was an agonizing moment when Marl began to realize that she wasn't going to say anything.

Afterwards, they went backstage to offer congratulations. Marl reluctantly handed her the potted hyacinth he'd bought. She didn't give them much notice. She was in mid-oration, and she didn't like being interrupted.

"Shakespeare's dominant passion," she declared, fingernails raised heavenward, "is, it seems to me, the very essence of the tragic spirit. Do you understand what I am saying? Shakespeare's essence . . . is . . . to hew out the man via a domineering psychology. Shakespeare's essence is his ability to provide a framework, around which the actor may place his drapery. Do you understand what I am saying? It's—" her hands flew out and cut a neat frame in the air "—it's that *initial* intensity . . . It's that dramatic movement of his—" her hands cut another neat frame, as if this one, finally, would capture Shakespeare's essence—"above all, it's that overwhelming conviction that there is purpose in pain—that out of the sand of agony—a pearl is born." And on this last note, her features, auburn-lined, began to blanch, and she seemed to transform herself into some grand statue, the moulded outpouring of some mammoth furnace of suffering.

"Let's get out of here," his father said.

"Hell, yes."

They left Marl to break into the circle of her listeners. Outside, the rain was coming down with a harder drive.

"Here," Ed said, tilting the umbrella, "you're saving too much of it for me."

"I'm great," Tom said, watching the signals change in the puddles.

"That place," Ed said. "It reminds me of a high school."

"Yes."

They looked at each other. Unsure. Ed started to shake with the feeling that his father could see to the bottom of him; and Tom, looking from behind his resistance, knew that this was not what he had wanted but that it had happened anyway. When Ed had first gotten home, he had felt nothing but a nerveless composure, but through nothing more definable than the answer and question of voices, he was finding himself changed, invested, once again in the outer world, and not just in the outer world but in his son. He looked back at his other self and wanted it returned. He feared this lack of detachment. But the alteration was permanent; the texture of his nerves had changed against his will and there was no way of reclaiming the earlier pattern; and here he was, set up, committed, all ready to be leveled again.

They spent the time before going to bed listening to the radio. Ed watched the city change within the Columbia. A

70 percent chance of snow, the weatherman said. A fresh storm for the Northwest. They decided to leave a little early the next morning and beat the change.

At 6 a.m., however, there was no sign of a blizzard. Only the rain of the night before, frozen slightly with the drop in temperature. Once they were out on the highway, winds zigzagged in front of them, stirring the random corners of snow like sand, but, still, there seemed to be no danger. It was not until they were 150 miles into the trip that the rain started to thicken, atomizing into a storm which whirled both sides of the road into ghostly tornadoes. The overcast split into tatters; hail and snow came at the same time; and Tom, sweating at the wheel, could feel the car swerve into twisted intersections of wind. On all the hills, the evergreens were lost in the coils of the blizzard; and in the car Tom and Ed both sensed the windshield loosening. They came to "Grade," and the car went rocketing downward, every frame of glass shaking. Tom braked—when he caught sight of the berserk truck. A sudden rotation of the steering wheel, when he found he could not brake and had to swerve on past. They took the turn, missed the truck, and hit three gales, descending from above like beams from heaven. The fingers of wind took the car, spun it 360 degrees, took them down four declivities of ice—like sledding trails, until they were finally set in a town.

Over grimy coffee and a linoleum-plated table, they waited out the storm.

THIRTEEN

Fenced outside the arena of the fourteen local boards, Ed filled his time by reading—"*New.* Civil Defense Air Raid Instructions. At home, at work, at school, outdoors. No warning—bright flash. Don't use telephone." The telephone which the placard presented was definitely 1950's, with the numbers drawn inside the holes, and a thick dogbone for a receiver. The placard's radio was of the same vintage, with Dick Tracy static coming out of its single speaker.

There were other helpful hints, like those he had gotten in grade school. "Don't let a fall spoil your future." "Bicyclists must use hand signals, too."

Also a message from the President, new by comparison: "Together we can move our nation on a road of unity and progress. New programs and policies must be applied to the pressing needs of today and tomorrow.

"The new leadership understands a great strength of our system; the dedication of governmental careerists to new policies and new directions."

He watched the women inside the arena. They moved back and forth with hot pitchers in their hands, disappearing into closets and conference rooms. Probably it was just coffee, but their mannered hurry made them seem like women of the cinematic frontier, delivering a child.

He pressed his palms against his slacks. He was all brushed and slicked up for his appearance, and he was bothered by the usual questions of hypocrisy. He tried to model himself after his father's composure, but he was always stopped by the knowledge that his father—at least in his new condition—would never have gotten himself into this. He would have taken the I-Y and left it at that.

Mrs. Jenkins, the local clerk, came to the gate and opened it. "They're ready for you now, Mr. Hill." She was enjoying her advantage and carried his file conspicuously. They went through an outer hall, out another gate and finally into a room which smelled faintly of rum maple tobacco. Unfortunately, the first man Ed looked at was Jamison Hanshaw. Jamison was immediately apologetic, but his pipe smoke was resigned. Next to him—Byron Torgrimson, presiding, surprisingly, over the meeting—as signified by his formidable reference materials. Then, Jim Sandberg, the medallioned college president, who seemed to promise he'd veto Torgrimson, if the younger became too compassionate—it was the way he was sitting. And then the usual assortment of men, more or less recognizable, Dan Samuels and Kenny Meyers, who tried to hide their anxiety and sympathy by frowning in desperate earnest.

They swore Ed in. Mrs. Jenkins wrote it down. Taking his seat, Ed had sudden designs on Jamison's life and immediately knew his anger was going to put him under.

Torgrimson went through his file, also a copy of Ed's C.O. form. By comparison, he was diligent and got through the routine questions with remarkable speed, never confusing them with the central issue, which he postponed.

Finally, he said, "I'd like to begin with some of the difficulties I have with your idea of religion, Mr. Hill. On page 2"—appropriate flutter of pages—"that your idea of God 'recognizes and forgives all men for what they are.' Does that mean that Christ makes room for a Communist?"

"He could make room for everybody," Ed said.

"What about the proverb," Torgrimson said, "of the sheep and the goats?" He was filling his pipe and looking theoretic.

"It doesn't make any sense."

"Why doesn't it make any sense?" Sandberg asked.

"I don't believe Christ would have said that."

"How do you know?" Meyers asked, eyebrows raised. "Have you talked with him recently?"

Chuckle—which more than encouraged Meyers.

"In other words," Sandberg said, "you believe—as far as the Bible goes—what you want to believe."

"I believe," Ed said, "what makes sense in light of what I know of Christ."

"How do you feel," Sandberg said, "about World War II?"

"I'm not sure I know."

"It's very simple. What would you have done if a madman was going around exterminating—people—and trying to take over the world?"

"I would try," Ed said, "to show him by my own example that his violent ways were wrong."

"Oh, come on, Ed," Jamison added good-humoredly, "I can't believe you would honestly sit down in the face of Hitler and everything he stood for?"

"I'd try, yes."

"Meaning you probably would," Sandberg said.

In the silence, Meyers worked up the nerve to speak. "Mr. Hill, do you hunt or fish?"

"Yes, I fish. A little."

"But if you hunt and fish," Samuels said, materializing at the far end, "how could you be a pacifist? How could you stand to watch the fish flopping, trying to get air?"

There were near-tears in his voice, and Ed was attracted. "I admit I don't like that part."

"Which part do you like?" Torgrimson asked.

"Eating it."

Laughter.

"I see," Torgrimson said, "you don't mind killing animals."

"Mr. Hill," Sandberg said, "what would you do if you had heard some maniac had raped your sister?"

"I would go and see him."

"What would you do, once you met him face to face?"

"I'd probably force myself to hit him."

"Does that make sense," Torgrimson asked, "in light of what you said about being a pacifist?"

"No, it doesn't," Ed said. "But I have been brought up in this country and that means that in order to act in accord with my background I'd have to hit the man."

"Why?" Torgrimson said.

"I don't know. I'd just have to."

"Then I don't see," Samuels said, "why you filled out Form 150." He still sounded on the verge of tears.

"I wish I could explain," Ed said.

"And if you do go out for hunting and fishing," Samuels said, "I don't see the sense in carrying this any further."

Still, Ed was attracted. Unlike Sandberg, Samuels had some shyness knitted in his brows. "What I'm trying to say," Ed said, "is that what I believe and what my background tells me I should believe are two different things."

Meyers asked, "What is your father, Mr. Hill?"

Ed drew a blank and stared.

"What does your father do for a living?"

"He's a retailer."

Jamison started to speak but stopped.

"Does he agree with what you've said here in this form?"

"No," Ed said.

"Why not?" Sandberg asked.

"Because he's gotten to the point," Ed said, "where he's beyond this kind of thing."

"Does he think you should accept your I-Y until further notice?" Jamison asked.

"Yes."

"Then your father believes," Torgrimson said, "that it is necessary to serve your country by aiding in its defense?"

"No," Ed said, "he's beyond that, too."

"But I thought you said—" Sandberg looked at Torgrimson with triumph "—that your background would tell you to hit that man who raped your sister."

Ed was exasperated. "When I say 'background,' I don't mean what my father tells himself—or me. What I mean by background," Ed said, "is . . . the moral weave behind the national identity." Utter bafflement. "It's what your father suggests is right when he doesn't even know himself that he's suggesting it."

Torgrimson was pitying him.

"That's about as clear as mud," Meyers said.

"Let's start from scratch," Samuels said. "What would you do if you came home and found some man raping your grandmother?"

"I don't think any man would want to rape my grandmother."

Laughter. Meyers didn't like being upstaged. "Smart ass?" —behind his fist.

"Getting back to the form," Torgrimson said, speaking loudly and admonishing the others, "you say that 'God to me is a perfect essence, absolutely good and all-eternal, expressed in the universe through the trinity. Christ was born out of this goodness so that he might become tangible to humanity.' Would you mind telling us," he asked, smiling, "what all this means in simple layman's terms?"

"Every man," Ed said, "is a trinity unto himself. As far as I can tell, every man goes through three distinct stages in his life: self-satisfaction, out-reaching, and loneliness. Exactly parallel to Father, Son and Holy Ghost."

Jamison: "Food for thought."

Meyers: "Clear as mud."

"But what does this have to do with your feelings about war?" Torgrimson asked.

Ed hesitated. "History has a pattern to fulfill; every man has the right to go through the three stages of his own trinity."

Sandberg shook his head. "You have nothing, then, in the way of a church?"

"No," Ed said. "This is what you'd call my own religion."

"Well, we can't give you a C.O. on the basis of that," Sandberg said.

"Not entirely, anyway," Torgrimson said. Sandberg glowered at him, clearly outraged at being corrected. Watching, Ed saw that Sandberg considered himself the true kingpin. Somewhere along the line, Torgrimson had put him down, and Sandberg had been planning revenge ever since.

Torgrimson added—fatally—"I'm sure we're all aware of the new rulings on personal religion."

Slants came into Sandberg's face, the first promise of an ambush— and not Ed's.

"You realize, of course," Meyers was saying, "that if we gave you the C.O., someone would have to take your place?"

"You mean," Ed said, "that even if I get the C.O., men will keep joining up and take the place I left vacant?"

"No," Sandberg said, "that's not what he means at all. We have a certain quota of I-A's to fill each month. I-A-O's will help fill the bill, but the I-O's don't count."

"Mr. Hill," Samuels said, "what religion is your father?"

"Methodist."

"Why aren't you Methodist?"

"Because I couldn't bring myself to believe in an exclusive religion."

Sandberg: "What do you mean, 'exclusive'?"

"Gentlemen," Torgrimson said, "I feel it is fairly clear that Mr. Hill has made his beliefs known to us—"

"Wait just a minute," Sandberg said irritably, "I want to know what he means by 'exclusive.' "

"I didn't think there was any need," Torgrimson said, straining against apology.

Silence. Ed waited. "I guess," he said, finally, "that what I mean by 'exclusive' is a religion that has damnation for some, salvation for others."

"But you say that you're a Christian," Samuels said.

"Yes."

"That's a laugh," Meyers said.

Ed was getting hostile. He knew he would lose if it happened—but there was no way of reversing the direction he was taking. "It isn't a laugh," he said. "I am Christian in that I believe in the ultimate goodness of love, of the need for God to be expressed in human flesh." Without the slightest bit of self-irony, he now hated every last one of them, perfectly. He couldn't quite see over the top.

"But do you believe in the crucifixion?" Samuels asked. He was being a purist again.

"No," Ed said, "I don't believe in the crucifixion."

"And you have no church affiliation?" Sandberg asked.

"No. And as far as I'm concerned, the church must die before we can have any morality."

Sandberg was leveled.

"Gentlemen," Jamison said, "I think we can straighten this thing out. Ed—do you believe in what we commonly call the resurrection?"

"I believe that one man's love for someone else may save him."

"You're hedging," Sandberg said. "Christ came into the world to save sinners—right?"

Ed half acquiesced.

"Christ came into the world to save sinners because there was an initial debt to pay."

The sound of the word set off a chain of alarms. "No."

"But you've got to believe it!" Sandberg said.

"No, you've got to believe it," Ed said, trying to control his anger while remembering what he'd heard about the college incident, and Sandberg's presiding over it.

"I think," Torgrimson began, "that—"

"Wait a minute," Sandberg said, "I'm not through. When I'm through I'll tell you. Now—I'd like to know from Mr. Hill here—who in fact admits in this very document that he took part in a violent demonstration—how he provides for forgiveness in this scheme of his."

"I haven't provided for it," Ed said.

"Yet you admit that you need it."

"Yes," Ed said—his mind skipped poles—"but not as much as you."

"What do you mean by that remark?" Meyers asked.

"I mean," Ed said, "that Dr. Sandberg probably makes peace with his conscience by thinking he's so thoroughly forgiven."

"That wasn't warranted," Torgrimson said.

The subordinates on the board—Jamison, Meyers, Samuels—huddled together. Sandberg was about to erupt.

"If you've got a charge to make," Sandberg said, "make it."

"All right—I think you skirt around the killings on your campus because you think Jesus loves you."

"There's no more need for this," Torgrimson said. "If there are no more questions, I'll—"

"Wait a minute," Sandberg said again, "if this is the actual kind of filth my students are spreading about me . . ."

Silence.

"Well, is it?"

"I don't know," Ed said, "it's what I think."

"I'd like to know," Meyers said, "just what makes you think you're such hot stuff." The atmosphere had changed. The meeting, for all practical purposes, was over. Still, Torgrimson didn't seem quite capable of ending it.

"I don't understand your question."

"Here you are," Meyers said, "enjoying all the benefits of this country and still you think you're privileged enough to refuse to serve."

"I'm not sure how many benefits this country has," Ed said. He was getting angry again. For the first time that he could remember, one siege was giving rise to another. There was no aftermath or release.

"There is no country," said Jamison, "with a higher standard of living. You know that, Ed."

"That isn't true, though. Denmark has a much higher standard."

"Have you been to Denmark?" Samuels asked.

"No," Ed said. "But I do know that they even keep their pigs clean there."

Another silence, with another huddling. It formed a zero. Ed, even through his anger, was starting to feel guilty.

"You're a very interesting case," Meyers said finally. "Not only are you proverbially snotty, but also you're one who thinks he's found religion. Most of our boys have some traumatic experience to tell us about, where they lost religion."

"If their religion was anything," Ed said, "they wouldn't have lost it because of one experience. That's nothing but mental melodrama."

Ed instantly felt the lurch, in Torgrimson. "Of course that's not true," Torgrimson said.

"Of course what isn't true?" Sandberg asked.

"He was saying," Torgrimson said, "that a man who loses his faith on account of an experience is necessarily weak. I was saying that of course that isn't so."

"Of course it *is* so," Sandberg said.

"No, it isn't," Torgrimson said. "There are some things in this life which give a man the right to forget the 'religion bit.' "

Embarrassed silence.

"Is there any final statement which you would like to make?" Torgrimson asked, turning to Ed and blushing.

"No," Ed said, "I'm through."

"That's for sure," Meyers said.

"Bit player," Ed said.

"Effete snob," Meyers said.

"Greasy has-been," Ed said.

"Smart ass," Meyers said.

"Dip-shit pig," Ed said.

"Snotty upstart," Meyers said.

"Shit-for-brains," Ed said.

"Gentlemen!" Mrs. Jenkins said, clearly horrified by her own shorthand. The intervention provided his exit. He moved from the room, the commotion having reached the outer arena through the open door. The other board clerks watched him as he passed their desks slowly, and he returned their stares, one for one. Each glance was rigid, frozen, and he was certain these women—all of them older than his mother—actually feared physical harm from him.

Then he was out of the arena. Yet already he could hear the board dispersing in the outer hall.

And he kept thinking about Ross. Ross of Pre-Induction, who had suggested what a farce getting a C.O. was.

Entering the waiting room, Ed ran straight into his father.

"How'd it go?" he asked, smiling.

"Terrible. I didn't get it."

"It doesn't matter."

"It does, though," Ed said, still persisting.

"All right." His father helped him on with his coat.

Then they both turned back. The whole troop was coming out. His father saw the face of Jamison Hanshaw and Jamison stumbled into the glance—his own gaze folding in on itself. Immediately Jamison was separated from the rest of the men, while Torgrimson and Sandberg were arguing.

"If I told you," Torgrimson said, "that some guy had come back from Vietnam and lost his religion, would you blame him for that?"

"I would," Sandberg answered.

And Tom, holding the door open for Ed and letting it fall on the others, kept watching Jamison through the glass and pinning him down. Then, placing himself between Ed and the whole re-emerging, top-coated group, he only said, "I'm surprised at you"—to Jamison mostly, even though each member clearly considered it directed at himself.

FOURTEEN

"Did Jamison give you trouble?" his father asked, when they were in the car.

"Not at all," Ed said.

"It's hard to believe he'd get himself into this. Especially with Sandberg there. He must be new, anyway. I hadn't heard about it before."

"Maybe he joined while you were sick," Ed said.

Silence—finally his father looked over. "So you're taking it in your stride?"

"No, I wanted to kill Jamison."

"But not now?"

"No."

His father didn't ask why and Ed was glad.

"How about Sandberg?"

"He's the one I still want to kill," Ed said.

His father nodded. "It was Sandberg and his gang that got me blackballed from the club."

"That's how I felt," Ed said. But he envied his father's confidence, his ability to remain whole after ridicule. He was so far from it. Each of the five members seemed to hold bits of him. Still, he couldn't ask his father, "How did you do it? How did you lay the cornerstone?" His father would only shy away, thinking he would be misleading, arrogant. But arrogance had nothing to do with it.

"How did you feel," Ed asked, "when you found out your club had dropped you?"

"Not too good."

"What'd you do afterwards?"

"Well—the mail came at noon, so I probably had lunch and worked."

Ed looked straight into the street, trying to decide what he would do next. Unless his board decided to make him I-A Delinquent, he was, for all practical purposes, free. He felt a strong closure, as if he and his father could calmly reject everyone else. But then, again, his energies were being turned in other ways, railing against his accusers as a whole, then creating separate mental portraits and trying to offer a rebuttal.

Visual jingle of Christmas light and traffic signs—the iceberg star dripping down six stories of the Bon Marche Department Store. The sound of traffic moved through the city like echoes through steam pipes. For a second, silver slippers spun in a window, beneath a tree of gold foil. Blue Ballerina Types. Here, here. The front of The New Washington Hotel was marigold, in neon. Cornucopia Room. Next door, there was the Stardust. They came to a crowded cloverleaf and waited. The lit cars moved in monotonous carousel.

And Tom, sitting at the wheel and watching, felt restless, hurried. "Let's get through this," he thought, "and then we'll be home. And once we're home, we can have dinner, and once dinner's over, we can talk, and once talk is over, bed. Bed, sleep, and then work. Some good work."

"What'd you do afterwards?" Ed had asked.

"Well—the mail came at noon, so I probably had lunch and worked."

And he knew it was not probably. It had happened that way. Exactly. After getting the mail and feeling he'd been stabbed in the back, he'd grabbed a tawdry sandwich and run out to the busline, all the while thinking, "Get your ass in gear. Chad's is falling apart."

And then he had wondered at himself, because there had always been the silent agreement that the store and its sales were never to be taken seriously. Chad actually got mad if you put the customer first. "Keep it schlocky, keep it schlocky," he'd say whenever Tom put in a window, and Tom would try to make it as ugly and tinkling as possible—one display after the next—but he always found a lurch in his hands, as if to set it right, instinctively—within the borders of taste.

And he knew that day, eating the sandwich on the busline, that he had to move, move because Ed's Pre-Induction had been two days earlier and Ed had gotten angry at the two of them, himself and Chad, during the dinner following; and the rise in his nerves had not spent itself, and already he was thinking of the windows on either side of the entrance, and of the two sleighs of reindeer which Haus's sold out by the old boarded-up Funland, where the cars of the Mad Mouse roller coaster still hung on the tracks, about to dive; with Tom thinking, "This is a day of hags. The hags'll be out, looking for bargains. All right, then, let's give them their money's worth."

And the minute he had gotten into the store he started browbeating Chad—"Come on, you've got to get them. Come on, Christmas is just around the corner."

"Let it stay there," Chad said. "Christmas is commercialized. Christmas disgusts me. Besides, if you want to get technical, it's too late, anyway."

And Chad went on counting the receipts from the drawer, but Tom pounded at him, threatening to quit ("O.K., Fine—quit. Just let me alone.") with the pressure rising and Tom insisting that he'd come back and bother him, even if he was fired, with Chad suddenly relenting and the two of them driving out after hours, all the way to the deserted Funland, where the roller coaster still stood arrested, just at the point where it had been before; where the Ichabod figure, set on top of the house, pointed across the road with globeless eyes, with the ferris wheel teetering on its hinges, and the voice still told the story that "the kid got so excited watching the girlie show, he shot off in his pants, so that the only thing he could do afterwards was get on the ferris wheel, to kind of dry things off." And the booths still advertised Coney Islands, Parachute Jumps, and Slush Sundaes, and the magician still did his hawking at the gate with "Watch closely!" and looking like a seagull with glasses or like Ichabod himself, or the dummy who dropped down on rubber bands and gave the girls a thrill in the spook house.

And then they finally came to Haus's, paid cash for the two sleighs and then drove all the way back and put them in the windows, on either side of the entrance, like bookends. And Tom rigged up a couple of strands of lights, which had been snatched up from the cellar, set tiers of turntables to rotating (slacks, slacks, sox, sox), so that by the time they left, he was thinking, "Tomorrow will be another day of hags, but this time we'll be ready for them."

And at that moment he regarded his creations, the two windows which were more like two theater marquees, pumping light through neon branches without spilling over, without turning into tinsel and trash. And he thought, "I will no longer call my memory trash. I will no longer be afraid of meeting Elden Foley on the street. What I said to them I won't apologize for. I'm not ashamed. I'll use what's happened. Use it."

But there was still the restlessness, even now, as the two of them, he and his son, passed through the cloverleaf and went home. He spent the night thinking of what he would do the next day, and when he awoke the next morning, he awoke remembering, again, that, rounding a corner, he had seen the sign—"Bellbuoy Tavern"—and the molten sunset through the windshield. And he awoke, thinking, "Today will be a day of hags," even as he dressed in slacks, clean shirt, cardigan, and jacket, hearing, to boot, a snatch of Dixieland that whistled like new flags above Funland.

"I'm coming over and shopping," Karin said at breakfast. "Today's my day off. So get ready."

"You bringing another offer from Jamison?"

"Shut up," she said. "And I'm going to bring Marl with me. We'll be helping out with the Salvation Army across the street."

"In the soup kitchen, Karin. You make the best turkey bone soup."

"You are a grand pain in the ass. Maybe I won't come and see you."

"If you don't," Tom said, "I'll refuse to be creative on behalf of my employer."

"As far as I'm concerned," Karin said, "there's only one way you could be creative with your employer."

"Give the cash box a shove?"

"Something like that."

She fixed his lunch and he went out running. At the store, Chad was testy.

"What do you want the ladder for?"

"Don't argue," Tom said, "go and get it."

"You go and get it."

"Then lead the way."

Still resisting, Chad kicked open the trapdoor, and they went down the orange-crate stairs. The supports protested, cursing the weight.

"What's this?" Tom said.

"A Pollyanna game. The owner before me used to give them out as prizes."

The boxtop had four figures on it, all in silhouette. The girls seemed to be shaking their tresses against a storm.

"And what's this?" Tom asked, still digging. He opened the top. A music box. The jingle sounded like the Marseillaise.

"That's mine," Chad said, suddenly.

"What's it doing down here?"

"I got it when I was in the service. It was made sometime in the nineteenth century. Now what do you want down here?"

Tom was still looking at the cherubs. "Some old ties. And some fake holly, plus the ladder."

They crept back up the stairs, tentatively holding everything. The supports' curse was double. Once they were above ground again, Tom started in on the four trophy heads which lined the far wall.

"What are you doing to my mooses?" Chad said, outraged.

"You just wait." He put the holly in their antlers, and then —tied ties around their necks. Windsor knots.

"You fucker," Chad said.

"What's wrong?" Tom asked. "No imagination?"

"You're demented. Utterly and completely demented."

Tom stood back, admiring. "No, I don't think so. In fact, I've got another idea."

But he was interrupted. A customer had come in.

"I need a belt for my husband," the woman said.

"Right over here." Tom twirled the rack for her.

"You look familiar."

"Sally Sivers?" he said.

Chad looked heavenward. "Shit."

"It's funny," she said. "I saw you on the bus just weeks ago, and before that it was five years."

"You still at Kress's?" he asked.

"Yes—terrific memory—still at the fountain. Bill's changed jobs, though. He's a bellhop at the Olympic."

"What was the matter at the Rutherford? Didn't he like it?"

"Fired," she said, "don't ask me why. And it did something to him. I only hope he stays with this one." She twirled the belts and took one at random. "This'll be fine," she said, not even looking at it. Tom brought it to the counter.

"$5.95?" he said.

"Oh, no," she said, going through her purse. "That's more than I've got."

Tom just stood there. "There are a lot of other—"

"No," she said, "I'll tell you what I'll do. I'll put two dollars lay-away and come back for it."

"That'll be fine—I'll have it wrapped by the time you get back. In fact, you don't need to leave any money."

But she handed it across anyway and dashed out.

Tom picked up the belt and dropped it, as if it were a dead snake.

"She won't be back," Chad said.

"I know."

Tom was starting to lose sight of his project. Karin and Marl came in.

"Wasn't that Sally Sivers?" Karin asked.

"Yes."

"She was beet red," Marl said.

"That was quite a low-cut dress," Karin said, sitting down.

"What'd she buy?" Marl asked.

"A jockstrap," Chad said.

Karin shook her head. "Doesn't he ever shut up?"

"What can you expect," Chad said, "when in you two come—demoralizing my help. You helping over at the Salvation Army bazaar?"

"Yes," Marl said.

"I thought so." Chad went into the back room.

"So, you going to come to lunch with us?" Marl asked.

"No. I've got this project I want to finish."

"That hardly sounds like you," Karin said, concerned. "You sure you're feeling all right?"

"Sure I'm sure."

"They serve great lunches at the bazaar," Marl said, wistfully.

"And they're going to have a jug band."

Tom cocked his head so he could see through the glass entrance. "I'd like to, but I want to put some lights in that tree outside."

"The City'll get you for that," Marl said. "I've tried it."

"That's my worry. You two go ahead."

"Are you sure you're O.K.?" Karin asked, staring. "You don't look too good."

"I'm fine. You two go ahead—unless I can help unload anything."

"No," Marl said, "we've already done that."

When they finally got up to leave, Karin kept turning around and staring. "I guess he's all right," he could hear her say.

He brought some other Christmas lights up from the cellar.

"Tom," Jamison said, entering tentatively.

He stood still, holding the heavy box tightly. "Come in," he said.

Silence. Jamison was rigid also, nervously eyeing the merchandise in the store.

"So how's business, Jamison? I hear you just opened in Jutland a few weeks ago."

"Pretty good—in fact, I could only dash out for a few minutes. So I could see you."

Still, the merchandise seemed to distract him.

"I know what you're thinking, Jamison. You're wondering how I could end up in a place like this."

"No, Tom."

"Well, I'll tell you—it's makeshift, but it'll do, it'll do!"

A woman came in. "Where are the people," she asked, "who are supposed to serve me?"

"Right here, Mam," Tom said. "It'll be just a minute."

And a salesman came in and stood waiting at the counter. Chad had disappeared.

Jamison looked meek. "I realize you're filling up," he said, "but I just wanted to see if—"

Tom frowned but nodded. He said, "Jamison, we tend to forget that I did you in. Maybe I'm the one who should be saying the apologies. I don't know about the board, and I don't frankly know what Ed will do—that's up to him. But if there have been any grudges, I don't see why there should be any now. So will you let me go, so I can wait on my hag?"

Jamison seemed satisfied with that but still hesitated. "I just wanted you to know I kept them from classifying him delinquent. He said some things, you know."

Tom nodded. "I know. I would have said them, too."

Jamison looked surprised again and left with only a partial wave. He disappeared before Tom got to his customer. "I want," the hag said, "some tennis shoes for myself."

"Why, of course, Mam," Tom said gallantly. "Yes, indeed, please step this way."

"I don't like," the hag said, sitting down in the wrong chair, "to sit next to dirty ashtrays."

"Of course, Madam. Of course. Now what color would you like?"

"What colors do you have?"

"Blue, lavender, denim blue, navy blue, powder blue, red, pink, celery, fuchsia, loden green, beige, leaf brown, yellow, sail yellow, white, and cranberry."

"White," the hag said. "I hate colors."

Tom went to the back room and found he didn't have her size.

"How about beige?" he asked, coming back with a box.

"I hate pointed toes. Show me beige in a rounded toe."

He went back to see if they had any. They didn't have any.

"How about leaf brown?" he asked, half-ironic.

"Let me see it," she said.

He brought out a fourth box.

"I told you," she said, looking at it. "I hate colors. And again, it's too pointed."

Tom went back and got her just the thing: a 1955 needle toe, in flaming lavender.

"How about this—Mam?"

"I'd take it," she said, giving it a thorough examination, "except that it's not my size. I take a six, not a ten.

"Oh, that's right—sure. Well, you stop in and see us next week. Maybe we'll have what you want then."

"Fat chance," the hag said, picking up her shopping bags. "Fat chance." She retied her kerchief and waddled out.

"Sorry to keep you waiting," he told the salesman, who was still at the counter.

"That's all right. That was quite a gem you had there."

"Get them all the time. I've had whole days of them. What can I do for you?"

"I was just wondering," the man said, "if you'd be interested in a new line of nylons. Something that's hot."

Chad appeared again—from the back: "No."

"You got a couple of samples?" Tom asked.

"Sure," stooping over his briefcase. It was the old style, with the tongue-lock.

"You're pretty young for that," Tom said. "That was made way before your time."

"Yes," the young man said, "I got it off somebody else." He stood straight, fanning out the pattern. "Here's the diamond, four ways."

Tom pressed the cellophane. Terrific style but cheap material. It'd sell fast but there would be a lot of returns—by which time the man could not be found.

"It is good stuff, but I guess we have enough already."

Chad was still listening from the back. "Thanks a lot, but good-bye. See you. Sorry to see you leave so soon."

The salesman's face took on a slant, which Tom recognized immediately. A diagonal of bravado which backs up against the first sign of ridicule, which carries men clear across the country, even in the face of clownish disaster.

"Wait a minute," Tom said, hesitating. "Would you like to sell these?"

"The samples?"

"Sure—you've got others, don't you?"

"Yeah—but what would you want them for?"

"My wife. My wife would like them."

"Sure," the man said, seeing through to the pity. "I'm just sure your wife would want diamond hose on her legs." He shut his ancient briefcase and swung it out.

Tom went back to his Christmas lights, tested two duds. Through the entrance he saw 1) a salesman throw his samples in the back of his station wagon and 2) the jug band arrive in front of the Salvation Army. Pretty soon he heard music. It united with the Dixieland he had been hearing in his head all morning.

"And everyone starts waiting for the vocal, with the double-down bass line rolling across the naked strings like thunder, and the drums start to pick up and everybody starts rocking in their seat, and the vocalist comes to the microphone, getting in rhythm with the drums, and then there's the backbeat of the piano again, and then the rising—this is what you've been waiting for—'yes—travelin' shoes!'—and the audience goes wild with her voice."

He took the ladder outside and started putting the lights on the tree.

He could still hear—even barring the music of the jug band—the tune that had come from Chad's music box, the Marseillaise, and he remembered the voice of a man he had encountered in a veteran's hospital, when the man had just been leaning against a window at the far end of the hall, and when Tom had passed, the man—short, in his fifties—had just started talking, switched on: "I should've gotten into something else, but I got into the War instead and we were stationed in France, and I went upstairs and I shouldn't have done that, but that's the way they did things in those days: she was a Frenchwoman and I went outdoors and I became a street urchin in Brooklyn and then I wouldn't've—"

And he thought, suddenly, of the waters separating France from Brooklyn, and then he was taken to a different vantage, he could see—watching the man's fingers pick out the rhythm—a town (either Watkins Glen, New York, or Monroe, Washington), could see a white-washed restaurant set out over the water, its windows filled with uncertain glass, ready to break like bubbles of glycerin, and he saw the cook hurrying through the kitchen, opening a drawer and finding a water rat; and he could see a statue of Joseph, his palms opening in the random snow, and he could see the railway crossings, with the cars passing over the tracks, with their transmissions thudding afterwards.

And in finishing his work with the lights, he started to rock at the top of the ladder, in time to the jug band music, hummed with the kazoo, and in coming down the ladder, he nearly pounced on the hag he had waited on earlier, the hag drawing back and saying—"You come down a ladder like that and you should have eyes in the back of your head," with Tom seeing himself round a corner and seeing the windows of Chad's store and saying "this is it," and regaining his composure all the while and saying to the hag with a tip of his hand, "Oh, Mam, I've got eyes in the back of my head, it's just that I forgot my glasses," and keeling over on the spot, saying to himself, "Why, I went down fighting," and finding, then, that he did not have time to laugh.

FIFTEEN

Ed awoke. It took him a moment to decide where he was. In that moment of an evening's dream, he remembered that he had ridden a bus through the city all that morning, had gone through the Fremont district, past Woodland Park, down through Wallingford and looping back, watching the people shift their Venetian blinds along Phinney Avenue, when the sun cut through the rain and startled them.

He awoke. In the half second of voyaging he also remembered that he had been sleeping hard, that he had let himself descend to the very bottom of the blue-lit evening, a fragment of exhaustion. And then he remembered that he had been listening, that the phone was ringing, that the alarm was sounding through him.

"Your father's just had a severe heart attack," his Aunt Ellen said. "He's at Jutland General now, and you should come at once."

"How is he?" Not yet awake.

"Critical." She still had the inevitable condescension of the bearer of bad news.

"Is Mom there?"

"She's with us. But you should come at once."

He hung up and got ready in five minutes. But half-way out the door, he remembered: the dog hasn't been fed. And it might be a whole day before anyone got back to the house. But then, his father might die while he was mixing up the food. Idiocy. Still, the dog might be forgotten, and the neighbors were away.

He called the dog up from the basement and fought back his playfulness. Going to the cupboard, he found that they were out of meal, and that he'd have to go out to the toolshed. His father might die while he was out there. Still, he'd already wasted so much time, he'd better feed him. He ran outside, spilled meal all the way back to the kitchen, got the dog fed, and was on the road in another ten minutes.

Outside, the city seemed simplified. There were no cumbersome details. Just one smokestack which connected to a long plane of cloud, radiant against the empty sky. All the intersections seemed to have caution lights—no red and green—and Ed remembered running through them. He passed the visored lamps of the wrought iron bridge, and was immediately entering the center of Jutland.

In the back of the hospital, he parked in the wrong place, and once he was out of the car, he took the wrong footpath. He ended up knocking at the entrance to an unopened wing. He clamored—still nothing. He saw three nurses in a street-level window and called to them, but still—nothing. They examined the room of the new wing, and then filed out, snapping off the fluorescent lamp. He tore around the side, falling down several times, hurtled a hedge of leaves, and found that he was in the garden of the old museum. He was surrounded by figurine trolls.

Another path led downward, onto a well-lit street, and there the entrance was, on the other side.

When he finally reached the seventh floor and found the waiting room, the first thing he asked Ellen was, "Has he died yet?"

"No, no," she said, whispering. "Of course not."

He went into the waiting room and sat next to his mother. She only looked absent and pale.

"I think you should go in and see Dad—first thing," she said.

Ed waited, while a nurse was told that the son had arrived.

"You should see his underwear," she said, pointing to a "Sani-Safe" bag. "It was sopped with sweat by the time the ambulance got him."

The nurse came in, led him beneath the globes of the hall. "Here," she said.

His father had been stripped, then laid on a bed with the sheet up to his nipples. Tubes had been inserted into his nose.

Ed took his hand.

His father smiled. "You're so cold."

Ed: "Everyone's fine."

"Good."

With his hands crossed in front of him, his father was rising into a concentration.

"Ed—"

Ed: "The dog's fine. I just fed him."

The nurse passed by the door, held up a finger: "One."

"Ed—"

His father was about to give him some message, a legacy, but when he finally said it, it made no impression.

Ed, thinking of the message—"Don't rush through your years"—said, "That's O.K., Dad, settle back."

But his father knew he hadn't been understood; Ed had let the language get in the way. Grabbing Ed's hand, he held it until their knuckles whitened.

Ed, holding his hand, kept moving up to the threshold and stepping back. "I love you." But he couldn't say it. The edge of infinity clamored for it; it was his one chance, but still the resistance in him asserted itself, and he was left mute, holding his father's hand.

His father saw the muteness in his gaze, acknowledged it with a mute sympathy of his own, and then eased back, released from the present.

The nurse came in and guided him out. Sitting next to his mother again, he knew somehow that his father was dead. His mother opened a Bible she had found there, and looked at passages. At about eleven, some interns rattled past, rushing his father down the hall in a sort of panic. His father's hair—brushed into a boyish bang—shook all the way, with the transfusion swinging like lanterns in a wind.

"Why is he all pale and white like that?" Karin said.

"He looks fine," Marl said.

"But he was all pale and white." She stopped a nurse. "Why was he all pale and white like that?"

"I'm sure," the nurse said, "that they're just moving him to a place where heart surgery is possible." But she felt she had said too much. "The doctor will be in to talk to you in an hour or so."

They waited, in silence.

Guiltily, Marl said. "What say you and I get some coffee?" He was looking at Ed.

"Will you be all right?" Ed asked, turning to his mother.

"That's all right," Ellen said. "I'll be here."

Once they were in the elevator, Marl said, "I feel terrible, but I really have to stop at the Men's Room. Is that all right with you?"

"Of course."

Once they were on ground level, Marl hurried in and out, as if his action would defile the dead. They went down a flight of stairs and got some coffee for the four of them.

"Dr. Starin still hasn't come," Karin said, when they returned. "Do you think I should stop another nurse?"

"No," Ed said, "it should be just a few more minutes." He thought of the fact, as if he'd remembered suddenly, and forgotten it, that his father was dead. He remembered the way his father had released his grip, like someone relaxing after exercise.

Dr. Starin came in, said, "We lost him." He sat down, bending a little. "We sure tried everything, but nothing worked. He was gone by the time we started the surgery."

Marl and Ellen gripped Karin at the same time. She said, "Keep your hands away, please."

A nurse came in with a release for possible autopsy. Karin signed them, in triplicate.

"You may see him, if you like," the nurse said. "But I will have to tell you, he looks very blue and discolored."

"No," Ed said, "she will not see him."

Karin broke, held onto Ed, who was struggling with himself as well. "I don't want to leave without him. What's the sense in going home?"

"He's with us," Ed said, sentimentally—because bitterness and regret were uppermost.

"That's right," Marl said. "And it's best we go home." But crying seized him, and he had to sit down.

Ed went over and helped him up. Marl put his hand on his shoulder. "I think you're right," Ed said. "We should get out of here."

They crept to the elevator, his mother leaning against him. Her muscles said she had given up; downstairs in the lobby, the switchboard operator deliberately turned her head, when she saw his mother. A janitor ran in front of them, afraid. Outside they agreed that Ed would take Karin straight home, and that in the morning they would get in touch.

Backing out of the lot, Ed put his arm around her. She was still saying, "There's no sense in going home."

And Ed, although he opposed her, kept feeling her insistence entering his nerves, so that he teased the cars which whisked past them.

At home, he helped her into the tub, but she simply cried into the water, her breasts sagging. "I never laughed at his jokes," she said, "and he always wanted to make light of things. Especially after he got fired."

Still unable to answer, he went out to the kitchen and made something for her to eat. Marl and Ellen shyly entered the house. "We thought we'd better come," they said. Ellen took over the kitchen and sent Ed back to his mother.

"Mom," he said—she had put on a robe and gone into the living room—"We'll manage. If I can, you can."

"What do you mean?" she said, angry. "Did you love him?"

"Yes," Ed said, "I did. I loved him more than any man." He hesitated. "Or woman."

She glowered. "But you never told him so, did you?"

"No. But men don't go around telling each other that."

"And that's why," she said, still frozen, angry, "there wasn't any love lost between you. Both proud to the hilt."

"That was true," Ed said, "at first. But not now—not later."

" 'Not now,' " she said. "What does that mean? Nothing. Just as he's nothing now."

They were silent. Without Tom, they felt ludicrous together.

SIXTEEN

Then it was time for the airport. As Marl and Ellen drove them out, Ed could tell that Karin was waiting: waiting for him to become a master over her. He answered by taking the sack from her lap, and immediately her eyes cleared.

"You don't have to keep talking," she told him, once they were on the plane. "No problem. I'm fine, I'm fine. Just put the sack—away. I'm fine, I'm fine—now read, now."

Ed put the package under his seat, and then—he had nothing else to do. The plane rose, and, breaking through the grey tissue, flew above high-floating, islanded clouds, with expanses of fields beneath. The lake streams were frozen into golden veins, and the ripples of mountain top were like shavings of pink ice. The webbing of frozen forests was still discernible, even at this height, their boughs as frail as flutes of chilled glass.

All Tuesday afternoon they had walked through the vault of the funeral home, searching for the right casket. Their satin centers had reminded Ed of jewelry boxes, encasements for the very fragile. The selection once over—they had gone upstairs to settle the details.

"I'll have three copies of the certificate sent to you," the Director said.

"Good," Karin said. "The insurance company wants it—and the hospital wants to be paid right away. I really don't have enough money, and I'm thinking of going to St. Louis to take Tom back."

"I see," the Director said. "What do you have in mind?"

"Well, there's a family plot back in St. Louis, and I'd like to take Tom there, just like he did his own dad."

"Well, Mrs. Hill," the Director said, "they just don't do that anymore."

They were all seated around his office—the buds of rhododendrons shaking against the window, their sheaths very yellow in the bronze light. Marl, brow-beaten by the expedition downstairs, had pushed himself against the book shelf, leaving his wife to sit by Karin. Instinctively, she took her hand when the Director squelched the idea.

Finally he said: "There are, though, other ways."

"Yes, cremation," Karin said, getting out with it.

"I think that would be very sensible" he said, relieved. "What do the rest of you think?"

"How do you go for it, Karin?" Marl asked.

"I think it's all right—Tom said once he wouldn't mind it —but I still want him put back in St. Louis."

"We could certainly arrange for that," the Director said. "We could have him shipped to whichever address you'd like, parcel post."

"I'm sure we wouldn't want that," Marl said. "Is there any other way?"

"Why," Ed asked, "does he have to be buried in St. Louis in the first place?"

"It's a part of the family plan," Marl said. "Tom always said so himself."

"When could the urn be ready?" Ellen asked.

"Anytime you like. Could we settle on Thursday?"

Karin, relaxing suddenly, said, "Yes—that will give me enough time to get the tickets and the packing done. Is there anything else?"

The Director, taking the cue, said, "No."

They all stood up and filed out, the Director holding the door open with his heels together. Ed, finding himself in the lead, stopped a moment to take his mother's hand and then guiding her out to the sidewalk, crossed at the intersection. The restaurant was on the other side. Scooting his tray across the stainless steel rails, he noticed that her glance was darting all over the displayed food, as if the proper things wouldn't be given to her. The worry was tightening her eyes and mouth again, and it carried through the cafeteria line, all the way to the cash register, where they couldn't find any cream for her tea.

Finally, they all followed Ed to the table, with Marl at the end. For some reason, he hesitated to take a seat. Setting down a tray which held nothing but a cup of coffee, Marl said, "I can't eat," and looked apologetic.

The plane descended, and they walked out into the St. Louis evening. His father's sister and brother-in-law met them at the gate. There was a suppleness that surrounded the couple, his uncle Chris looking well-chiselled and free of antique frost. For the moment, his Aunt Ann seemed less defined.

"We heard from Eleanor Vance," she said, once they were in the car. "It came just when Tom was written up in your paper there. She sent the clipping."

"Marl wrote that," Karin said. "Ed, do you have the sack?"

"Yes."

"Marl wrote that. It was very good, I thought. Ed said he just couldn't do it."

"That makes perfect sense," Ann said, waiting for her. When there was silence: "Eleanor Vance is out here now, and she's one of a few people who'll be there tomorrow."

"I hope there won't be too many," Ed said.

"No, just Eleanor and a few other people."

"But don't we just want family?"

"Well, yes," Chris said, above his driving. "But there aren't an awful lot of relatives still living. We didn't think you'd mind if we asked some of our close friends."

"No, we don't," Karin said firmly, and she seemed to hand out a note of moralizing. Ed, sitting back and waiting, guessed he was being obtuse. Still, it was hard to believe that his father's memorial service was going to be just another obscure funeral, attended by distant relatives and coaxed friends.

"Is Elden Foley going to be there?" he asked finally. "I really don't want him to be there."

"Well, that depends," Chris said. "Technically, anybody can come who wants to—"

"Does he know?" Ed asked.

"I'm sure the whole Company knows," Chris said.

"And I'm sure they're weeping bitterly."

"Ed—" his mother.

"No," Ann said, "they're not bitterly weeping. But Foley might feel some regret for firing him. And if he shows up tomorrow, that'll be the reason."

"If he feels regret," Ed said, "why doesn't he get his company to send Mom more money?"

"I don't want more money," Karin said, hostile. "And I don't see why you have to spoil everything that Chris and Ann have done."

"I'm not spoiling it. I just don't want some kind of wholesale floor show tomorrow, where any curiosity-seeking hypocrite can stick his nose in. I still say Dad ought to have been buried in Jutland."

"That's a rather awful thing to say now that we're here," Karin said. "And it's a rather awful thing to say about Chris and Ann's friends."

"I don't mean their friends, goddamn it. I mean Elden Foley. Do you think Dad would have wanted him to come?"

"I don't know," Karin said. "I don't know what he would have wanted, and I don't see how you think you know either."

Silence.

"We have just about everything ready for the dinner," Chris said, "except for the meat. We called for it, but we'll have to stop and get it."

Backing into a bronze alley, they stopped before a cold lattice of iron. Ed, getting out with his uncle, noticed, for the first time, that St. Louis was thirty degrees colder than Seattle.

"It's an old place," Chris said, holding the door for him. "I bet it's been awhile since you've seen sawdust floors."

The visceral smell was sudden. Until then his throat had been dusty with the smell of airports—Sea-Tac and O'Hare, where they had transferred—now trays of chops and sirloin, set beneath light and glass, seemed like the work of a remarkable craft. The butcher, still friendly after eight hours of work, was bloody but neat, and the cut of ham which he handed Chris had been prepared like the rest. It was a cut, not a slab.

"About Foley," Chris said, pausing on the sidewalk. "What he does or doesn't do—I think—isn't up to us, unless it intrudes."

"But as far as I'm concerned," Ed said, "he's just raking in part of the glory of paying homage to Dad, when really he's just lying through his teeth."

"And you think stopping him's going to do some good?"

"It'll cut him down to size—it never hurts when somebody's got it coming."

Chris only looked at him, then got back into the car.

At their house, Ed found a small living room of the 1920's, with coal-dark registers. While Ann made dinner, Chris got firewood from a leaf-covered bin in the toolshed. Ed, following, was still afraid to pick up their conversation and silently watched Chris make the fire: with thin pieces of plywood he first built a tent of flame; then intermediary wood came next, and finally a block of cedar.

At dinner, they talked some of his father, but Ann and Chris seemed to move the subject away from him whenever they could—not out of fear of the dead, Ed decided, but out of a refined acknowledgement of the living. Taking their lead and yet still not fully understanding, Ed found himself returning to his child's question of what his grandfather was like.

He had gotten up and was whacking the fire through the parted screen. "What about that family heirloom—the bookcase?" he asked. "I always liked it, but where was it before it got to Seattle?"

"Well," Chris said, "we had it here for about fifty years, or anyway it seemed like it, and it was right over there, taking up a corner of the living room. And when Edward finally asked for us to send it, we had to spend about two days just packing it to make sure the glass wouldn't break. And of course it did break."

"The way his return letter sounded," Ann said, "you would have thought we'd taken great pains to kick through every frame before we'd shipped it."

"It seemed like in his memoirs he died embittered," Ed said.

"Embittered—no—disappointed—yes," Ann answered. "He should have been a gentleman farmer, a scholar farmer. But the two sides never quite held together."

"What about the *Litra Primer*?" Ed asked.

"That was his last and best effort—as far as publishing went."

"You mean there were a lot of other things?" Ed asked. "Other things besides the memoirs?"

"Yes, some of it's in the family Bible," Chris said. "We'll get it out after we've had some coffee."

And so, when all the dishes were cleared, Ed lingered over the book, while the rest watched the news. At the back, there was a bound leaflet entitled "Poetic Occasions," and the first entry was an elegy, written by his great-grandfather.

To James Hill, aged sixteen, died of a fever.

Blow ye winds and gently hover
O'er the grave that hides my Brother
For thou wilt soon blow: over another
Perhaps before tomorrow at noon.

While on his deathbed He was dying
And his parents round Him crying
Brothers and Sisters by Him sighing
Jimmie thou wilt leave us soon.

The embalmed diction—the well-meaning landscaping—but then again there were the facts of the poem, a glimpse of Jim, whoever he was, lying on a bed; and even more, a glimpse of his own great-grandfather, sitting at a writing desk, trying to write a poor tribute.

"Memory Springs"—Edward Hill to his wife.
When far away from her.

What magic hath the odor of a rose,
That it can conjure back a day long gone?
Doth witchery caged, that falling flakes
Do cast a spell of youth o'er age and youth wan?

The weakest blossom of a tardy Spring
Doth typify the faith in which we rest;
A summer-time of purest joy enfoldeth while
The blue-bird twitters on her nest.

By narrow windows thus we stand, betimes,
To contemplate some vast expanse of plane,
Where like a mountain mirrored in a moat
The lesser seems the greater to contain.

1914

Nor was this the historical moment he'd been waiting for; he had always hoped to be nudged by centuries, but not this way: and already he was feeling himself being bound up—in the traditional coils of a carefully preserved bad taste, extending all the way back to his first well-meaning and pious ancestor.

And yet—he admired it. The utter nerve to write something so disastrously bad and believe in it. Like his father before him, Edward Hill, Sr., had lifted his winged fancy to the occasion and had fallen splendidly, catastrophically. Alongside their ingenuous efforts, his own refined abstinence seemed pale. It had been his Uncle Marl, then, who had taken up the legacy, writing his father's commemoration as the occasion demanded. They, the three of them, had achieved something.

Afraid of showing his emotion, he quickly shut the leaflet.

They rode out to the cemetary early. Streams, frozen to isinglass, crossed the tawny knolls and ended in opaque pools. Because of the cold, Ed and Karin waited inside the caretaker's cottage while Chris and Ann went to check about the canopy and chairs.

They sat for a moment in silence, then Karin took up the sack. "Would you mind opening it up?" she asked, handing it over. "I'm sure they'll want it for the ceremony pretty soon."

"Sure. But do you want me to go outside and do it?"

"No," she said, looking away. "You know that doesn't bother me."

He removed the box, broke the seal. His mother saw Tom's name on the urn and broke down.

For the moment, he did not intrude upon her, but remained quiet. Finally he said, "It should start pretty soon."

"That's right."

They watched as enamelled flies climbed the walls.

"Do you have your suitcases packed?"

"Yes."

"How about the plane?" she asked. "Did you check?"

"It leaves at 8:45—and Marl and Ellen will be there to pick us up."

"I may not go back with you—at least not as far as Seattle."

Ed turned to her, surprised. But there wasn't time to ask what she meant—people were starting to come in—close friends, they said, of Ann and Chris. Two women, one old and one young—probably mother and daughter—took some seats at the back. They did not try to make conversation but sat, simply, with their hands folded. Chris finally entered, followed by a series of men and women who spoke nervously about a new viaduct. As they talked, the mother and daughter still sat separate from the others, submitting to silence.

"I have a new reconciliation," Ed decided. And as he sat with the urn in his hands, he seemed to hear some Latinate lines, spinning out of darkness, where short vowel and long vowel, long vowel and short vowel, fused all beginning and endings; rushing, endless, ceaseless, like a waterfall or tidal line of waves, the great begetting and re-begetting, where leaves flowered out of ashes, flowered and withered down into coals again.

His mother started to cry.

His aunt returned.

They all stood up and walked out, one by one. The path led high over the crest of a knoll, and they walked, a meandering line, very slowly, avoiding the glassy rills. When they reached the canopy, a portable heater took the frost off their glasses, and soon the minister was ready to signal Ed: put the urn here. He arose and did so, and as the minister said, "Oh Lord, let thy guiding hands receive the soul of thy servant Mr. Hill into thy bosom of rest," a clanking device lowered the urn through a trapdoor of artificial grass: Blow Ye Winds and Gently Hover.

But Ed, watching the urn clumsily disappear, saw into the betrayal of his reconciliation, and felt again the magnetic love for the atoms that had whirled into oblivion. Something collapsed and the urn was lost from view. Ed broke down and sobbed bitterly, not because the fact of death crushed him but because he was too fully aware of his failure to show love to another man. He stiffened under his tears and forced them to stop.

Seated toward the back were two men, one of whom he recognized as Jamison Hanshaw, the other he decided—because of the artfulness of the clothes—must be Elden Foley. Ed wiped his eyes. His mother, observing his recognition, said, "Be careful," also through tears. But Ed, calmed now, found himself able to bide his time.

The service over, he led the procession out and gave his

arm to his mother, when she was drawn to turn and look at the receding canopy. It wasn't until the group had reached the cottage and nearly dispersed that he finally removed himself from her and walked up to Foley. "Please leave," he said.

Foley's face fell for a moment, and then he was out on the walk, heading for the parking lot. Before he was gone from view, Ed had confronted Jamison also and said the same.

Chris and Ann came up from the back and called after him, but Jamison only waved from behind the car window and drove off, following Foley at a close distance.

"You've done nothing—" Chris said, coming back.

"They needed to be excluded," Ed said.

"Not Jamison," his mother insisted, coming up. "How could you do that? He wanted to pay his respects to Tom by speaking to us. And all had been forgiven before Tom died."

But Ed, too overwhelmed by his failure, did not listen. He said—to all of them—"I don't want Dad buried here. We have to take his ashes back."

Ed sat waiting at his Uncle Marl's counter. The clerks were having their morning coffee while the customers banged to get in.

"You been seeing that draft counselor again?" Marl asked.

"Yes."

"How's it going?"

"O.K. Nothing's changed, though. I'm still a C.O. that my draft board won't recognize."

"Is that counselor pushing you toward prison? This would be a perfect chance to."

"Not that I can tell—although I think he's heading that way himself."

"Just don't let him take you over."

"I won't."

"You coming by tonight—for supper?"

"Sure—if it's O.K."

"Got a letter for you—from Shirley."

"Thanks. I think I know what it says."

Other clerks were joining them.

"The customers want in."

"Let 'em wait," Marl said. "They've got all month for this sale."

Orlaf the butcher was just standing there. "Rain drove out my freezer," he said.

"Jamison Hanshaw died."

The women were handing a baby around.

"The rain drove out my freezer."

"Yes, Orlaf, we heard you. Now come and have a cup of coffee."

"So Jamison Hanshaw is dead."

"Jamison Hanshaw? I thought he was too mean to die."

"He wasn't mean," Ed said.

"Well, I don't have any tears for him," Marl said.

"Why not?" Florence asked—she was behind the fountain.

"Oh, he thought he was pretty hot stuff, and he didn't know crap about business."

"Of course he didn't know crap about business," Florence said. "He was a school teacher. And a good one. I had three kids go through his home room, and he was good and learned to every one of them."

"Learned, my foot," Marl said. He whispered to Ed: "And he tried high-hatting me everytime I saw him."

"Oh, it was Latin grammar," Orlaf said, with supreme resignation.

"*Dominus Vobiscum*," Maury, a clerk, said. "That's what I'd say if I went to his funeral."

"Shut up," Florence said.

"So Jamison Hanshaw is dead."

"I was very mean to him—"

"Shut up," Maury's kid sister said.

"Who's going to get his store?" Mabel said.

"His store?" his uncle asked. "It's been gutted from top to bottom. That 'drastic sale' he had to go through."

"Ed—"

"You can't hold *that* against him," Florence said.

"Who said I did?"

"Then what have you got against him?"

"He was a fuss-budget," his uncle said. "He was always on you while acting like he wasn't."

Ed checked the time. "I've got to get a move on, if I'm going to get those windows done by two."

"Don't rush," his uncle said, "take your time."

"I've got that other work I'm doing so I better. I've got to bone up if I'm ever going to get back in school."

"You're coming for supper though?"

"Sure—thanks."

"You've got to, because today's your birthday."

"O.K. Thanks."

"Hey," Marl yelled. "Everybody—today's Ed's birthday."

"Yeah?"

"Oh, it was Latin grammar!"

"Prick," Florence half whispered to Maury, "how could one man have so many mean things to say about the dead?"

"So Jamison Hanshaw is dead."

"Got to get going," Ed said. "And do those windows."

"O.K., O.K."

Ed got into the showcase of the storefront windows. Embracing the life-sized Easter Bunny, he danced it through the back entrance, finding a place in the corner and wrapping it in a sheet of plastic. Out in the showcase again, he watched while slants of ultramarine flashed in the overcast like lit waves, then vanished in the swells of tumbling cloud. Stretches of shadow hovered below the ceiling like massive butterflies. The sun came through the apple-green glass, disappeared, returned.

The letter—his mother was not coming back. Not now. Not later. She was having nothing more to do with him, or with anybody else. She was cancelled out, complete, free to move into the city of the Ocean. There was no need to read further; Shirley would always say the same things. His mother was there to stay.

Coiling up the last of the trimming, he locked up the cases and went out through the back. A mist was rising up from the waters and gardens which rimmed the whole circle of Jutland, a languorous cloud, which turned dim, along with the smoke of the lumberyard. The people had their lunches—there was a flap of curtains from The Bell Apartments—and the overcast shut out the sun.

At the end of the street, a man, the Jack-of-all-trades, got out of his Studebaker and started pulling boards from the entrance to the Jutland theater. Coming to the crosswalk, Ed felt the whole district lie heavily at the base of him, not because he had smoked and eaten too much, loafed and drunk too much, but because he, like everybody else, had worked too hard—become worn. And in a few hours, when he saw the draft counselors, they would begin the next segment of their plodding track of alternate scorn and reconciliation, Ed trying to tell them that despite his failure he was still a Conscientious Objector, and the counselors trying not to show that they owned nothing but contempt for a C.O.—a dodge from prison—whether acknowledged or unacknowledged by his board. And they would go through the motions of their chase and subsequent truce-making—with Ed returning, again and again, to the belief that prison—in his life—would be worth nothing if done by way of martyrdom. And that night, after a brief visit to the Jutland cemetary, he would go to the chateau of his uncle and aunt's apartment building, and she would serve him coffee and cake with Danish paper napkins, and they would ask him back again, because they knew he loved them more than anyone else, for they were among the last he could love.

Finding himself in the dead center of the district, he heard a roar of traffic wave over, forming an eddy. Quits. Selling Out to Bare Walls at Wholesale Cost or Less! Starts Thurs., at 9 am. Open Thurs. and Fri. til 9 pm. Oxford Specials $3.88. Men's Quality Edison Temps $6.88. Flats and Stacks. $2.88.

Ed looked again. It was Jamison Hanshaw's place, the fiasco he had started the year before, the last will and testament of a Latin teacher who preferred reading Virgil and

Boethius to advertising nylon hosiery. Hanshaw, Hanshaw, Hanshaw's, in neon, unlit. Ed tried to peer through the glassed front, but it was papered over. Stepping back, he forced himself to remember his mistake—of excluding him from the funeral—the man who had flown all the way from Seattle to St. Louis just to commemorate his father. Why? He checked his watch. 3:59. Why? Mothers Look at This, Hundreds of Pairs of Nationally Advertised Shoes. Jamison: had grown tired somewhere along the line of reading *The Aeneid,* had fitted out his store, gone bankrupt, and then quietly kicked the bucket. There was an adjustment in the traffic of the avenue. The shops lit their signs, like cars at dusk, answering one another.

He knew it was his failure—that had been his reason, his ploy. Exclusion was supposed to be a sign of protection, of love. Values Too Numerous to Mention. And his failure faced him like a grinding irony in the street.

"Ed—don't rush through your years."

And he had stood there, unable to answer.

He stood at the window. A day had passed—Jill, his friend, leaving his bed at noon. And now the day was moving on to four o'clock, and he must get on across town to teach his evening class at the bottom of this winking, changing city. Here is a Roman aqueduct, here is a Gothic cathedral, here is an old stone house—

And he repeated the configurations to himself as he went out, bereaved, into the Jutland dusk. He went along the street of seaview homes, where the crews had just broken ground for the new designs—some of them his own—but even the smell of sawdust and the sight of lumber could not cure him, could not heal.

Beyond, in the crosswork of shadows, beneath the foliage of clouds, was the cemetary, where finally he had laid his father to rest. And while his mother had fled to her own city, in search of her own memories, taking the LITRA PRIMER with her, his father had become a part of the deeply rooting mountain ash, while all the time the row of Jutland houses grew, their windows taking in a slice, a view, of the great broad waters, resting there like an extended acreage which belonged to them, within his design, and, previously, originally, his mind's eye, while his mother, first as a silhouette and then a ghost, moved along the high boulevards of the other city, beneath bay windows, through sandstone vaults, to an older vision, of close-packed houses, arranged in arcs, the courtyards lit by lanterns, their afterlight on the windows of restaurants, scrolled with the plush of curtains, the surrounding sites squared off in darkness, as she moved up streets lit by spheres of clouded glass—BALBOA POLYTECHNIC—AN ACCIDENCE FOR THE STUDENT PREPARING FOR HIGH SCHOOL AND COLLEGE—distracted by setting moons and flowers given speech, the old schools a collection of saw horses and broken tracery, and the palms containing the last glow of the sun the way a candle holds, cups, its flame.

But what the hell was this? For Ed, having visited his father, had come back into the district. Here, on the street, the Jack-of-all-trades was again pulling the boards off—this time of Jamison's dead store. Feeling Ed pause and watch, the stranger, the new entrepreneur, looked up, as a flame responds to a tentative wind. Keep-your-crap-shooting-eyes-off-me-you-bastard-and-don't-ask-me-why-I'm-doing-this-because-it's-none-of-your-fucking-business-see? And Ed, heartened, turned away, thinking again of Jamison and his mistake. Maybe there was excuse, apology, exoneration.

Crossing the street, he was stopped dead-center in the district by a vision of the city southward. It was 4:00, 4:00. And, three miles away, the city—the evening—was already changing, and he could feel the Showbox Theater, dead now for years, send out a puff of evening confetti not far from the Atlas Pool and Theater, Showbox Theater, SHOWBOX THEATER/Adults Only/please/please/please, and memory spun uncertainly around a rim, as a gyroscope spins tentatively around the lip of a jar and ValuesTooNumerousTo Mention and already he could hear a flap of ragged wings off the top of Wymansales—What? What—his father—his father —his father!

And the evening was changed.

Randy Kalisek

Henry Alley, born in 1945 in Seattle, now teaches in the English Department at the University of Idaho, where he is active in the creative writing program. He received his B.A., with honors, from Stanford; his M.F.A. in creative writing and his Ph.D. in prose fiction are from Cornell. His fiction has appeared in such journals as *The Virginia Woolf Quarterly, University Review, Webster Review* and *Cimarron Review.* He is author of the recently published *York Handbook for the Teaching of Creative Writing,* and his critical articles have appeared in *The Midwest Quarterly, Greyfriar: Siena Studies in Literature, Iowa English Bulletin* and the *Rocky Mountain Review of Language and Literature* (forthcoming). He has completed three other novels, *At Large, Umbrella of Glass* and *The Skeleton Crew.* His fifth novel is now in progress. Henry Alley has been an NEH Fellow and is a member of Phi Beta Kappa. He lives in Moscow, Idaho, with his wife Patricia and his daughter Ann.

Design and production of
Iris Press, Inc., titles
are under the direction of
Stuart McCarty,
The Geryon Press
Tunnel, New York.